## *"I think I may be falling in love with you,"*

Patrick said in a tone that stated and questioned at once.

"I . . ." Mitch wondered and doubted and told herself not to but ended up with, "I think I may be falling in love with you, too."

The admission was somehow freeing, cleansing, as if facing it took some of the ominous part away. Maybe she'd lost her mind, or the wine had gone to her head, but at that moment she wasn't worried about the future, about the pain she would suffer when she had to leave him. At that moment she could only bask in the feelings.

"What are we going to do about it?" he asked in a quiet, raspy voice.

Again Mitch surprised herself. It all seemed so clear, so uncomplicated, so unthreatening. "You could make love to me."

Dear Reader,

Welcome to the Silhouette **Special Edition** experience! With your search for consistently satisfying reading in mind, every month the authors and editors of Silhouette **Special Edition** aim to offer you a stimulating blend of deep emotions and high romance.

The name Silhouette **Special Edition** and the distinctive arch on the cover represent a commitment—a commitment to bring you six sensitive, substantial novels each month. In the pages of a Silhouette **Special Edition**, compelling true-to-life characters face riveting emotional issues—and come out winners. Both celebrated authors and newcomers to the series strive for depth and dimension, vividness and warmth, in writing these stories of living and loving in today's world.

The result, we hope, is romance you can believe in. Deeply emotional, richly romantic, infinitely rewarding—that's the Silhouette **Special Edition** experience. Come share it with us—six times a month!

From all the authors and editors of Silhouette **Special Edition**,

Best wishes,

Leslie Kazanjian,
Senior Editor

# VICTORIA PADE
## Something Special

*Silhouette Special Edition*

Published by Silhouette Books New York

**America's Publisher of Contemporary Romance**

**Books by Victoria Pade**

Silhouette Special Edition

*Breaking Every Rule* #402
*Divine Decadence* #473
*Shades and Shadows* #502
*Shelter from the Storm* #527
*Twice Shy* #558
*Something Special* #600

## *VICTORIA PADE,*

author of both historical and contemporary romance fiction, is the mother of two energetic daughters, Cori and Erin. Although she enjoys her chosen career as a novelist, she occasionally laments that she has never traveled beyond Disneyland, instead spending all her spare time plugging away at her computer. She takes breaks from writing by indulging in her favorite hobby—eating chocolate.

# EXTRA! EXTRA!

HEAD OF HALVORSEN GROCERY STORE EMPIRE
MISSING
Foul Play Suspected
—*Minneapolis News*, September 13

NO CLUES FOUND IN DISAPPEARANCE OF
HALVORSEN HEAD
—*Minnesota Post*, September 14

RANSOM NOTE BRINGS FBI INTO HALVORSEN
DISAPPEARANCE
—*St. Paul Sentinel*, September 15

SALE OF HEARSE LINKED TO HALVORSEN CASE
Authorities Lose Hope of Finding Grocery Head Alive
—*Twin Cities Times*, September 16

DISTRAUGHT HALVORSEN HEIR CHARGES
AUTHORITIES WITH INCOMPETENCE
Hires Private Investigator
FBI refutes claim: "The Halvorsen case is still
under investigation," says bureau chief.
—*News Today*, Minneapolis, October 25

# Chapter One

Hey lady, is that a hearse?"

Michelle—Mitch—Cuddy unlocked the car door and opened it. "Not anymore," she answered the group of teenage boys gathered outside the convenience store. Next door was the office of the answering service where she had been employed for the past three weeks.

"A pink hearse. How gross," Mitch heard as she got in.

She rolled her window down to let the barely cool night air in, started the engine and let it idle while she reached for a barrette on the dashboard. Aided by the bright outside lights of the convenience store, she looked into the rearview mirror and gathered her hair up off her neck. Too red, too curly, and in the late June heat spell that had hit Denver, too long. Leaving her hair down in the air-conditioned office was one thing, but for the ride home even at eleven at night, that would be like wearing a wool blanket around her shoulders.

There was a dark ink smudge on her nose and she rubbed it, sneering at her own reflection. Okay, so the nose wasn't so bad, not too long, not too short, not too wide, not too thin, not too pert. Just a nose, plain and simple and straight. But her eyes—why couldn't they have been emerald green to go with the red hair? Instead they were black. Coal black. Did she just think *red* hair? In spite of her mother's and Hilly's rebukes that her hair was not orange but deep burnished red, she'd always thought it looked orange. Orange hair, black eyes. Halloween.

And her cheeks. She blew just enough air into them to fill them out. What she wouldn't give for full ones rather than the hollows left by cheekbones that seemed to her to be too prominent. The slight concavity was one thing at thirty-three, but if they sunk any more—the way Hilly complained they did when you got older—she was going to have to go around with walnuts stuffed in them.

"Oh, well," she muttered to herself, realizing that she was just in a foul mood. Putting the hearse into reverse, she ignored the gawking stares the pink car drew as she swung out of the parking space. She headed for Bowles Street to get home—or at least to the place she and Hilly were house-sitting.

Once in the stream of traffic she reached over and turned on the radio. Hard rock assaulted her so she switched stations. Then she tried a third and a fourth before deciding everything grated on her nerves, and turned it off.

What was wrong with her tonight? she wondered. She had been antsy and uneasy this whole Friday evening.

Was it just jitters because one job was ending before she had another one lined up? No, she didn't think so. After three years of odd jobs and temporary employment, she was used to irregular sources of income.

Was it this house-sitting job?

Maybe.

Not that house-sitting was a source of anxiety or work she and Hilly hadn't done before. Actually it was the perfect arrangement for them. It gave them free room and board without the hassles of a lease to break if they needed to pick up and leave on the spur of the moment. It was also something Hilly had a knack for digging up for them. At seventy-eight the friends she made in each new city were usually retired. Among them was often a well-heeled one or two who traveled and could use their service.

"So," she said out loud to herself. "What has you as edgy as a candy fiend in a dentist's chair?"

Hilly and Alfred was the next thing to pop into her mind. Maybe it wasn't the house-sitting itself. Maybe it was the owner of the house and his relationship with Hilly.

Hilly had been seeing the debonair Alfred since just after she and Mitch had moved to Denver six months ago. Lately the elderly couple had been nearly inseparable. Not a good thing. For both Mitch and Hilly, forming attachments to people—especially men—could be a dangerous pitfall. The last thing they needed were ties of emotions binding them to places where they couldn't stay. And more and more it seemed as if Hilly had formed an attachment to Alfred Dangelo.

Yet for some reason even that didn't quite seem like the cause of this niggling feeling. Still, she decided that she and Hilly should have a talk about the lack of wisdom in the older woman getting in any deeper with Alfred.

Mitch turned into the driveway of Maplewood Estates, a cluster of enormous, elaborate homes that nestled behind an eight-foot brick wall. After two days of house-sitting, the security guard recognized her car. He waved and had the mechanical wrought-iron gate halfway open before Mitch pulled up alongside his brick booth. Distractedly she waved back and drove through, turning left. One block past the entrance she turned right onto Alfred's street. Her heart nearly stopped. At the opposite end were the flashing red and blue lights of police cars.

It wasn't Hilly and Alfred making her uptight, she realized in an instant of panic, it was a premonition. Somehow she always knew when things were on the verge of blowing up, when their past was about to catch up with their present. And there it was, she thought, in flashing, living color.

Biting her bottom lip, Mitch inched up the street, her mind working a mile a minute as she tried to think of what to do. Were the police looking for her?

"Well, you're easy enough to spot in a pink hearse," she said to herself.

Instantly she pulled over to the curb, quite a ways from the commotion up the street.

*Think, think.*

She could see neighbors in nightclothes and robes huddled in the yard and on the sidewalk in front of Alfred's redbrick three-story Georgian house. Mitch hadn't met any of them so she realized they wouldn't recognize her on sight. The car maybe, but not her. Quickly she got out, closing the door quietly so as not to draw any attention to herself. She rounded the hearse and ducked behind a tall row of evergreen trees. Better to come up on the group as if she had just left one of the other houses. Time was what she needed. Time to find out exactly what was going on, to see how best she could help Hilly.

Staying behind trees, shrubs and cars, she stealthily worked her way up past Alfred's house. Then she stepped out from the shadow of ivy-covered lattice that fenced a swimming pool, and took the cobbled walk from the front of the house to the curb as if she had just come outside.

Voices on police radios disturbed the quiet of the night. The rotating beacons on the cars threw glaring light like buckets of water flung out into the street. Mitch bit her bottom lip and pushed up the long sleeves of the white T-shirt she was wearing with blue jeans and tennis shoes.

There was a tall, serious-looking man heading purposefully toward Alfred's house from the property around the curve. He was dressed in a red polo shirt and black tennis shorts, and approached the group with something that seemed more than the mere curiosity of a bystander. Mitch hoped that meant he knew something. She crossed the street to intercept him.

"What happened?" she asked.

He stopped in his tracks and turned only his head her way. Milky light from a street lamp illuminated strikingly handsome, very angular features. The momentary dip of his chin told her he took a quick assessment of her. Then he frowned suspiciously. "Who are you?" he demanded authoritatively rather than answering her question, as if he would only impart his information to her if she proved to be someone who had the right to know.

Mitch swallowed but met his glance evenly. "I'm..." She hated herself for the split second it took her to come up with a lie. "I'm visiting my grandparents," she finished, keeping her fingers crossed and hoping that he wouldn't ask who among the many elderly people owning houses in Maplewood Estates those grandparents might be.

He didn't. Instead he said, "I see. Well, I'm not sure what's going on." He nodded back over his shoulder at the house around the curve, a sprawling Tudor-style ranch with a steep thatched roof. "I just drove up myself a few minutes ago. I'm Patrick Drake," he said as if that would prompt her to give more details about herself and where she belonged.

But at that same instant another police car arrived and Mitch's attention followed it. *Hang in there, Hilly, I'm coming.*

"I said, my name is Patrick Drake," he repeated, walking alongside Mitch as she inched her way deeper into the crowd.

That made her glance at him again. "Oh. I'm Mitch—I mean Michelle Cuddy," she answered, preoccupied.

"Al's not home, is he?" a woman just to Patrick Drake's right asked the tall man.

He paused to talk to her and Mitch kept on going, hoping to garner more information from someone else. It was then that she saw the ambulance that was at the very head of the driveway.

Heart attack. Hilly had had a heart attack, Mitch thought, going cold inside. No matter how vital and vibrant and healthy Hilly seemed she was still nearly eighty years old. Mitch fought the urge to rush to the house. *Don't cash in on me, Hilly. Please.*

"There's been talk of UFOs." It was Patrick Drake's voice—a low, rich bass. He fell in beside her once again.

"UFOs?"

"Margaret McFarley just said the police were called with a report of a Peeping Tom or a possible burglar and now the woman inside is claiming she saw a UFO."

That sounded like Hilly. Mitch released a breath she hadn't realized she'd been holding. The elderly woman must be all right. And if it was Hilly herself who had called the police—though Mitch couldn't imagine that she would—it meant the authorities weren't here looking for either of them. It was safe to go in.

Relieved, and without another word to Patrick Drake, Mitch left him behind and made her way quickly through the curious onlookers. She came face-to-face with a short, stocky policeman standing sentry at the carved double front doors.

"Excuse me, but I'm staying here with Hilly Nolan. We're house-sitting," she informed him.

The officer frowned at her.

"I'm Mitch Cuddy," she offered.

That seemed to ring a bell because the man pivoted around and held the front door open for her.

It struck Mitch that this was like something out of the movies. She went in to find two more policemen standing on either side of the arched doorway that led from the chandeliered foyer into the elegantly formal living room. Neither man so much as dropped her a glance as she walked between them.

For a moment Mitch stopped just inside the doorway. Hilly's first action whenever they arrived anywhere was to take over a spot for her grandfather clock—the only thing in the world the older woman truly cherished. In Alfred Dangelo's house that spot was a corner directly opposite of where Mitch was, and at that moment everyone in the room was standing around Hilly as she polished the clock as if everything else was inconsequential.

At barely five feet tall the thin, agile elderly woman was dwarfed by a very impatient-looking officer who stood somewhat behind her, holding a pencil poised over a clipboard so tightly that his fingers seemed bleached white. To Hilly's left were two white-garbed paramedics. One of them was taking her blood pressure while the other was making notations on yet another clipboard. The second paramedic was trying to suppress a smile as Hilly, in a scratchy voice, recounted the episode that had apparently brought them all here.

"Yes, I can see it clearly now. It was a small craft shaped like a spider. It hovered just outside the sliding glass door that opens onto the patio. I was sitting in that wing chair reading and I suppose I must have dozed off. You know how old ladies are, catnapping all the time."

Mitch suppressed a smile. Hilly had never taken a catnap in her life.

"It was that humming sound that woke me," she heard Hilly go on. "Then I saw the lid pop open on the spaceship and out floated three little bodyless heads shaped like eggplants.... Yes eggplants, that's it. They were eggplant people. The pupils of their eyes were that same dark purple color and their irises glowed yellow. They came right up to the glass, bobbing out there like soap bubbles and just staring in at me with their eggplant eyes in their eggplant heads." Hilly effected a shudder that sent her white cap of curls shimmying. "Well, that's when I called for help."

"Mrs. Nolan," the policeman began, obviously trying to be patient.

"*Ms.* please. I may be along in years but I'm a liberated woman."

"Blood pressure's normal," the paramedic said to the room in general.

"*Ms.* Nolan, we've checked all around the grounds and there isn't a sign of anything. Even the cobwebs in the basement windows are still there. Maybe you were just having a dream."

"Oh, no. I'm quite sure it was real. Why—"

Mitch decided it was time to step in, before Hilly got any more outrageous. "What's going on here?"

"Mitchy! Thank goodness." Hilly spun around to face her, giving her a quick wink that no one else could see. "We've had a terrible fright." She grabbed Mitch's left arm as if it were a lifeline.

Mitch introduced herself. The policeman turned his attention to her as if Hilly were a child he was grateful to no longer have to deal with. He explained that they had been called in on a report of a disturbance but since there was no sign of anything he felt sure Hilly had had a delusion. Then the paramedics chimed in with their judgement that she was not suffering any physical distress.

"I'm afraid Hilly is prone to very vivid nightmares, aren't you Hilly?"

The elderly woman pretended she hadn't heard. She let go of Mitch's arm and went back to polishing her clock intently. When Mitch realized Hilly had no intention of answering she said, "She must have dreamed this whole thing."

The police officer nodded his acceptance of that idea, his expression clearly showing sympathy for Mitch's association with the deranged old lady. "Then if you think you can handle things here, there's no sense in our staying any longer. We've done about all we can.''

"We'll be just fine," Mitch was quick to reassure. "I'm sorry for the trouble."

The paramedics packed up their equipment and left, but before the policeman followed them he turned a frown on Mitch. "Maybe in the future she shouldn't be left alone," he suggested.

"You could be right," Mitch agreed just so he'd leave.

He cast another disturbed glance at Hilly's back, said good-night to Mitch and finally headed out.

With the click of hard-soled shoes on the tiled entrance floor Hilly glanced over her shoulder at the departing policemen. Mitch wondered how anyone could look into the older woman's bright, sparklingly alert blue eyes and think she didn't have all her wits about her. But the authorities had apparently also missed that mischievous slant to her mouth and the ornery upward angle of her pale brows that would have told them she was making the whole thing up. Then, again, Hilly was wearing large gold hoop earrings, a long tank top over black spandex tights, scrunched up leg warmers around her ankles and jogging shoes. Mitch had to admit that Hilly didn't look much like a normal, sedate, stable, elderly woman, either.

Hilly faced her clock again to hide a soft, satisfied laugh that only someone as near as Mitch was could hear.

"You're a devil, do you know that?" Mitch said to her back. "What on earth were you doing getting the police here?"

Flicking her dust rag, Hilly spryly swatted a speck off the base of the clock. Then she turned around and started to say "I didn't—" But she stopped short when something behind Hilly caught her eye. "Oh. Hello."

Mitch looked over her shoulder. The man she had spoken to outside was standing in the doorway, watching them both with what appeared to be a very serious interest.

"I slipped in as the police were leaving," he offered by way of explanation but without the slightest hint that he had hesitated to come in or felt the inclination to apologize for it. He crossed over to Mitch in long strides of muscular legs, appearing very sure of himself. And very suspicious of them.

"Patrick Drake, wasn't it?" Mitch said in a confident voice that belied her internal disquiet over what he might have overheard or why he was there.

"Right. From next door," he reminded.

He folded his arms across a chest too broad to be ignored and Mitch's gaze somehow got stuck on the bulge of his biceps from beneath the short sleeves of his polo shirt. She dragged her eyes upward and found him looking around the room assessingly. Since he still wasn't offering a reason for being there, Mitch explained to Hilly. "I met Mr. Drake outside. He was the first person I came upon to ask what was going on." Then she tried to retrieve his attention with an introduction. "This is Hilly Nolan."

Patrick Drake had the good manners to stop scanning the room and look at the older woman. Hilly stepped right up to him and held out her hand. "So you're Patrick Drake. Well, isn't this nice? We finally get to meet."

For a moment he didn't say anything. He only inclined his head in a way that looked as if he was questioning something. Now that he was out of the shadows of the lamplight Mitch was struck by just how handsome he was. His dark brown hair was short, the top casually swept back and to the side. His eyes were deep set and a pale, pale blue that seemed almost translucent. His nose was long and straight above a thin upper lip and a fuller lower one, and just off center in his chin was a cleft.

So absorbed was Mitch with the sight of him that she was only peripherally aware that he had turned to her and was speaking. She reclaimed her senses in a hurry and concentrated on what he was saying.

"Funny, but from the way you walked up to me I had the impression that you had just come out of the Murphys' house across the street."

"Oh, well, I had to park my car and walk up, what with all the people and the police and everything," Mitch hedged.

"When you said you were visiting your grandparents I just assumed that would be the Murphys." He took a second sweeping glance around the room. "Where is your grandfather?"

Mitch was struck speechless while her mind raced to find an answer to cover her tracks. It was a nonplussed Hilly who interceded.

"You must have misunderstood, Patrick. May I call you Patrick? Wonderful. And you'll call me Hilly, everyone does. Of course Mitch must have said her grand*mother*, meaning me. She's keeping me company."

Patrick Drake's eyes had been boring into Mitch. She was grateful when he looked at Hilly. "Where is Al?"

"A golf tournament in Palm Springs. You've been away, too, haven't you? Alfred told me."

"I've been in New York since spring, yes." He frowned at Hilly. "I don't mean to seem rude, but who are you?"

Hilly laughed and slapped air. "That isn't rude. You must have left town just about the time Alfred and I met, so of course he wouldn't have told you. We're...well, at our age boyfriend and girlfriend seems absurd, so let's say we're seeing each other. And while he's gone, Mitch and I are house-sitting for him."

Patrick Drake looked dubious. "I've lived next door to Al for nearly eight years, we've been friends just as long, and I've never known him to hire anyone to house-sit before. Our security system here is usually enough protection when someone is away. In fact, Al sometimes doesn't even bother to lock his doors and I have to come over to do it for him after he's gone."

"Did you think he had hired us?" Hilly asked. "No, he insisted that we enjoy his home while he was gone. How could we refuse? Being house-sitters was just what we tagged it."

Mitch could see Patrick Drake was still not convinced. But by then she had regained some of her own composure. After all, most of what Hilly had said was the absolute truth and there was nothing about their being in this house that had to be hidden. "Alfred left a number where he can be reached. If it would make you feel more comfortable you're free to call and talk to him."

Patrick Drake's gaze slowly pivoted her way. "It isn't that I don't believe you, but I think I'd rest easier if I took you up on that."

While he made the call and Hilly put away her dust rag and furniture polish, Mitch went to the sliding glass doors and looked outside. The uneasiness she had felt on the way home was still with her in spite of the fact that the incident with the police had proved to be nothing threatening. She was itching to talk openly with Hilly and find out what it had all been about, but she had to have privacy for that. She wished Patrick Drake would take those amazing eyes and that big, hard, masculine body of his out of here.

The sound of the phone being hung up brought her around to face him again just as Hilly reappeared.

"Well, I feel a little stupid," he said with a charming, self-deprecating smile that made faint lines bracket his mouth and crinkle the corners of his eyes engagingly. "Al assured me you two are who you say you are. In fact, I've just agreed to keep an eye on you while he's gone."

"Isn't that nice," Hilly said, her tone genuinely pleased.

It didn't leave Mitch feeling the same way. For some reason this man made her intensely uncomfortable. "We do just fine on our own."

"Oh, no Mitchy, we can always do a little better being looked after by a nice man like Patrick."

So much for Hilly's being a liberated woman. Mitch pulled her shoulders back as if calling this meeting to a close. "Well, I'd better go bring the car up."

"I'll walk with you," Patrick said.

"Oh, no." She reacted too quickly, too loudly, she realized. But Mitch had intended this maneuver to get rid of him and all she could think of was that she had parked much farther away than she would have needed to simply avoid the crowd and police cars, and in the opposite direction from which he had seen her come. She amended her tone to sound casual. "It's no big deal. I'm sure you want to get home. It's late, after all, and Hilly and I are just going to lock things up and call it a night.''

''I can't have you out alone in the dark with UFOs lurking around and me having given my word to Al to watch over you,'' he insisted, teasing.

''There's no need. Really. None at all.'' Too quick again. She was beginning to sound panicked. She was beginning to feel panicked. There was something about those bare, tan, hairy legs of his and those thick forearms and wrists, and those penetrating eyes that caused goose bumps to erupt all over her just by being pointed her way. . . .

Hilly was no help. ''I'd feel better if you weren't out alone, Mitchy,'' she said pointedly and with a high arch of her fluffy eyebrows that told of a reason she couldn't go into at the moment.

Patrick seized Hilly's support. ''Then it's settled. Hilly was been upset enough tonight. We don't want to cause her any more uneasiness.''

''And I'll have brandy waiting when you get back. A nice nightcap will relax us all and seal our new friendship,'' Hilly finished.

With her face turned away from Patrick, Mitch narrowed her eyes at the older woman to relay how little she appreciated this. But with no other recourse she gave in.

The neighborhood was asleep again when Mitch and Patrick went out the front door. Patrick headed in the direction from which she had come. Mitch cleared her throat and pointed. ''It's this way.''

He pulled up a little short. ''But you came from the Murphys.''

''Yes, well. I wasn't thinking too clearly. I guess I just stopped the car the minute I saw that the commotion was at Alfred's house, got out and ended up walking all

the way past before I found a break in the crowd." It
was a feeble lie and she knew it. "This way," she blun-
dered on, heading down the street.

He caught up with her in two strides, falling in beside her on the sidewalk. "I suppose everyone reacts to
a scare differently. If I had come home to something
like that I would have charged like a bull to get through
to find out what was going on."

The sidewalk was narrow and, for some reason, being
that close to him made the already warm air seem hot-
ter. Mitch stepped down into the gutter to get farther
away from him, and stumbled. Patrick caught her,
grabbing ahold of her arm to keep her from falling.

*Inhale, two-three-four, exhale, two-three-four,* she
told herself. Not remembering how to breathe just because he touched her was a bad sign. Mitch tried to get
control of her senses.

"Whoops," was her only comment on her lack of
grace. It didn't make her feel any better to realize she
hadn't been able to say that until he had let go of her
arm. Determined to get far away from him, she made
another attempt at leaving the sidewalk, this time successfully.

In a rush to keep him from pursuing the subject of
why she hadn't gone immediately through the crowd to
Alfred's house she said, "Are you sure you don't have
to get home to your wife?" Okay, so she had been
wondering.

"I'm not married," he answered her with a smile in
his voice. "Are you?"

"No." She hadn't meant it to sound so curt, but she
didn't like being transparent. "You know this really
isn't necessary. Why don't you go ahead and go home."

He frowned at her for several steps. "I don't think you should hold it against me because I had to check you out. I know most of Al's friends and relatives, so when I didn't recognize you... Well, you could have known the house was vacant and taken it upon yourselves to move in for a while. It happens."

"I'm not holding it against you."

"It sounded like you were. Or do you just not like my looks?"

There was that disarming smile again. Mitch sighed and said honestly, "It's been a tough night."

He conceded that and nodded his head. They fell into silence for a few moments before he laughed and pointed with his chin. "Now that monstrosity has to belong to somebody visiting. I've never seen it around here before. What would possess anyone to drive a pink hearse?"

Mitch closed the distance to her car. "It's *my* monstrosity."

He groaned and grimaced exaggeratedly. "I'm batting a thousand tonight."

The pained look on his face made Mitch smile and relax a little. She took pity on him. "It's all right. I'm not crazy about it myself. But Hilly won't go anywhere without her grandfather clock and there's no other way to cart it around."

"Have you considered buying her a wristwatch?"

Mitch laughed. "Many times. She won't hear of it. Anyway, this is an improvement on the way the car was when we bought it. It had western boot decals and Urban Cowgirl painted all over it before."

In the dark glass of the windshield she caught sight of herself and blanched. She'd forgotten the barrette that still held her hair up. A split second later she wondered why it should matter how she looked. But it did.

She resisted the urge to take the barrette out and finger comb her hair. No big deal, she told herself. This was just Alfred's neighbor. So what if he was great-looking, charming and smelled of a wonderful spicy clean after-shave? "Get in and I'll drop you off at your door."

"And cheat me out of my brandy? Not a chance."

It had been worth a try. Mitch slid in behind the wheel and watched as Patrick went around the front. An image suddenly flashed through her mind of a "Where are they now" magazine article she'd seen not long ago. One of the men had been a terrific looking guy dressed in black leather, straddling a motorcycle. Patrick Drake reminded her of the man who was now a male model in Europe. Then he slipped into the passenger seat and she remembered to start the engine.

"So," he said as she pulled away from the curb. "Are you from around here?"

"Oh, not really. Well, yes, I suppose you could say that. We've been in Colorado for the past six months anyway." She was glad the drive to Alfred's house was much quicker than the walk.

"Who's we?" he asked.

"Hilly and me."

"You and your grandmother moved here together? That's unusual."

Mitch pulled into the driveway and turned off the car. "Still suspicious?" she challenged as she got out.

"Occupational hazard," he admitted, coming around to her.

She skirted the tiled fountain that spilled water for ceramic birds to bathe in, and headed for the house. "What's the occupation?"

"Originally I was a newspaper reporter."

Mitch stopped short. It took Patrick a few more steps to realize it. Then he turned back to her with a curious expression. But once more Mitch was saved by Hilly when the older woman opened the front door with a "There you two are. I was beginning to wonder."

A newspaper reporter. A newspaper reporter. It kept playing over and over again in Mitch's mind as she followed Alfred's neighbor into the house. But, she remembered, he'd said originally. Maybe that meant he wasn't one anymore.

Once a snoop, always a snoop, she argued with herself. Was there no end to the surprises tonight?

In the living room Hilly handed Patrick a brandy snifter and waved him into a chair. Mitch perched on the arm of the couch and tried hard to appear as if this piece of information hadn't shaken her.

"So how old are you, Patrick?" the elderly woman asked bluntly as she brought Mitch a brandy and then sat on the opposite end of the couch.

"Hilly," Mitch gently berated.

Patrick held his snifter up, laughing slightly. "Old enough for this but I'll show you my ID if you want."

Hilly laughed unabashedly. "Oh, come on. Everybody always wonders about everybody else's age. You look at me and wonder just *how old* that old broad is. Well, I'm seventy-eight. And I'm looking at you thinking you're around mid-thirties—just a little older than Mitchy's thirty-three. So why not ask outright?"

Mitch cringed inwardly. Ever since Hilly had found romance with Alfred she had been sounding more and more like a matchmaker.

Patrick didn't seem to notice. "I'm thirty-six."

Hilly snapped her fingers. "Wonderful. Married?"

"No!" Mitch blurted out in reflex. She had meant *no, don't do this* but that wasn't how the elderly woman took it.

"Oh, so you already asked."

Mitch closed her eyes and groaned. When she opened them it was to find Patrick watching her. Very slowly, he smiled in a way that said he understood how Hilly's bluntness was embarrassing her but not to let it bother her.

The answering swell of warmth and appreciation Mitch felt was unwelcome. Trying not to appear too pointed and wanting to change the subject, she said, "It seems our neighbor here is... was... a newspaper reporter."

"Is that so?" Hilly seemed enthralled. "Alfred told me you were his golfing partner but he didn't say anything about what you do."

"I *was* a reporter. I can't really claim that now."

"What are you now?" Mitch asked.

"I own a couple of magazines. At the moment I'm starting up a new publication called *Probe*."

"*Probe*," Hilly repeated. "That sounds very serious. What are you going to probe?"

"It'll be a monthly magazine concentrating on articles of an investigative nature."

A sip of brandy went down the wrong way and Mitch coughed and coughed until Hilly got up and hit her hard on the back. "Isn't that interesting?" she heard the older woman say over her head.

For the second time that night aplomb was hard to recover. Mitch put a concerted effort into it. "A newsmagazine? I suppose you'll aim for political transgression, breaches in national security, corporate corruption, major wrongdoing like that?"

"Actually we're looking as much for human interest—or I should say human injustices—as we are the bigger scopes. I suppose this comes from my hippie days, but I became a reporter in the beginning to cast light in shadowy corners. To bring truth and justice for all," he said theatrically, laughing at himself. "*Probe* is my baby in that way. I want to take up big causes and little causes alike and really make a difference."

"Through disclosure," Mitch said, unable to keep a critical note out of her voice.

"That's where it all begins."

His unusual eyes locked with Mitch's for a moment before Hilly said, "I think it's a terrific idea."

It was Patrick who broke the connection to grin over at Hilly. Obviously delighted by her, he teased, "I was hoping the UFO claim might give me the article I've been looking for to launch the magazine."

"You want to investigate my dreams?" she asked eagerly.

"Speaking of dreams," Mitch put in, standing suddenly. "It's been a long night and I think we could all use a little rest."

Patrick stood and set his snifter on the wet bar. To Hilly he said, "She's been trying to get rid of me all night. I think you really shook her up." Then he winked at Mitch. "Okay, this time you win. I'm going home. But first you and I need to make the rounds and check every door and window in this house so we all know this place is locked up tight."

"That isn't necessary. I'll check everything myself."

"I insist."

By now Mitch knew that arguing the point would only prolong his stay and, for more than one reason, she wanted him gone—out of the house, out of her life, so she could stop being so affected by him. "Let's do it then."

Besides the sliding glass doors in the living room, there was one in the formal, peach-colored dining room, another in the bright silver-and-white kitchen, and French doors in Alfred's book-lined den.

"You're sealed in down here, now let's go upstairs," Patrick said.

"With these high ceilings the windows on the other two levels are so far up it would take a human fly to get to them," Mitch pointed out.

"Or flying saucers," he said, as he waited for her to precede him up the stairs.

Together they tried the windows of all three bedrooms and the recreation area on the third level. Then, finally, they went back downstairs. From the entranceway Patrick leaned in to see if Hilly was still in the living room. "Good, she's gone." Then he turned those alarmingly penetrating eyes of his on Mitch. "Is she going to be all right?"

Mitch rubbed the goose bumps off her arms. "Hilly? Doesn't she seem all right now?"

"Does she do this often?"

"Have vivid dreams, you mean? Well, yes, but this is the first time she's called the police over one. She must have just gotten more unnerved than usual. But there was no harm done."

Still he stared at her, his expression showing genuine concern—and something else. Something that looked like appreciation. "What about you?"

"Me?" Why had her voice cracked?

"Are you okay? You've had quite a scare yourself tonight."

"Oh, I'm fine. Just fine. Nothing to worry about with me."

Still his eyes stayed on her, making her intensely uncomfortable. "You're sure? You seem on edge."

"Positive. I just need some sleep."

"All right. I'll check back with you tomorrow. If you need anything in the meantime, or if anything happens, I can get over here faster than security or the police. My number is programmed into Al's phones, all you have to do is press a button. It's listed on the console."

"Thanks, but I'm sure there won't be any need." Mitch opened the door.

"Good night, then."

She murmured a good-night of her own, closed the door behind him and locked it. The second she did a long wolf whistle sounded from behind her.

Mitch turned to find Hilly slinking down the hallway from the kitchen. "I didn't think he'd ever leave," she told the older woman.

Hilly laughed melodiously. "We both knew that, Mitchy. You were a little obvious."

"I don't care. The last thing we need is to get friendly with someone who makes his living *disclosing* things."

Hilly fanned her concern away. "He seemed like such a nice man. And attractive. Didn't you think?"

Mitch frowned at her. "That doesn't matter."

"No, of course it's what's inside that counts. But it sure helps when the packaging looks like that."

"You know what I mean, Hil."

"I think he liked you."

"I don't care." She was getting goose bumps. Maybe she'd caught a virus.

"I think you liked him." Hilly made a fist and jabbed the air toward Mitch with a thumbs-up sign. "I say relax and enjoy his attentions."

"No one says he's going to show me any attentions and if he did I could certainly not relax and enjoy them, for crying out loud. You know that."

Hilly swiveled around the newel post and started up the stairs. "It'd be good for you, Mitchy. A little flirtation. A little romance. A little sex . . ."

Mitch turned out the lights and followed Hilly, smiling in spite of herself at the older woman's back. "Didn't anybody ever tell you you were supposed to stop thinking about sex after seventy?" she teased her affectionately.

"You never stop thinking about it, Mitchy my love. That's how I know you ought to smile in the direction of our Mr.-Patrick-Drake-Fine-Speciman-Of-A-Man and see what you can heat up."

"You're incorrigible."

Hilly swept theatrically into her bedroom, leaning far back, her arm trailing behind. "I know."

"What on God's green earth happened tonight?" Mitch asked from the doorway.

"It's too late to go into all of it now. I'll tell you tomorrow. First thing in the morning."

Reluctantly Mitch conceded and said good-night. Then she went into her own room where the image of Patrick Drake followed in spite of herself.

## Chapter Two

Patrick was up early the following morning. It was good to be home after nearly five months in New York straightening out the mess of his latest acquisition—a financial magazine that had been on the verge of bankruptcy. But with that running smoothly now he could concentrate on *Probe*, headquartered in Denver.

Barefoot and wearing only an old pair of yellow tennis shorts, he went from the cream-and-cocoa-colored master bedroom at the back of the house, down the hallway, and around the sunken living room into the kitchen. "Coffee beans, coffee beans," he said to himself as he searched. "Ah, good girl, Nora," he breathed when he found them.

The house was spotlessly clean, the cupboards and refrigerator well stocked. In a call to his secretary at the *Probe* offices last week he had inadvertently complained about coming home to a stuffy, dusty house and no food. She had volunteered to take care of it for him.

He ground the beans, put the coffee on and opened the French doors that led out to the pool, letting in fresh morning air. Then he picked up the receiver of a state-of-the-art slate-gray telephone, pushed one button to dial and took it with him across the blue marble countertop to the oak dining-room table where his briefcase sat open.

"'Lo," was how his call was answered on the other end.

"You may have been instrumental in launching more than one newspaper and magazine for Drake Publications, Les, but I frown on editors-in-chief who sleep late in the morning," he said as he opened the briefcase.

"Paddy, me boy," Les Burns responded happily, if a bit thickly.

"No one with a Texas drawl should ever try an Irish brogue."

"What the hell do you expect when you get a man up at…" The sound of his long-time friend scrambling for a bedside clock came over the wire. "At six forty-three on a Saturday," he finally finished. "When did you get in?"

"Last night."

"Why didn't you call me? I would have picked you up at the airport."

"I did call you. I got some syrupy sweet little voice telling me *LB* was in the shower. I figured if you had female companionship for the night I wasn't going to interrupt it." He paused a beat and then added facetiously, "LB."

"Give me a break," his friend groaned.

"Are you alone now or is Miss Sweetness and Light lying there next to you listening?"

"I'm alone."

Patrick just laughed. With the phone held in place by his shoulder, he went to pour himself a cup of coffee. "So tell me you've come up with the story of the century since I talked to you two days ago."

Les groaned louder. "I wish I could."

"What about the tip that funds for the homeless were being extorted?"

"Nope. By the time our investigator got there the guy had been arrested. It's all taken care of and he only got away with about three hundred dollars—nothing big enough to give us a launch angle."

"It doesn't have to be big so much as it has to be a grabber."

"I know, with just enough scandal to attract attention, like a juicy high-society murder. Sorry, but no cigar." Les cleared his throat. "Speaking of high society, how are you doing with the news of Amy Rogers getting married?"

Patrick pinched the bridge of his nose and closed his eyes for a moment before answering. "She made it, didn't she? An oil tycoon. The wedding pictures were in every paper and magazine I've picked up in the past week. If I had known beforehand I would have warned the guy."

"Is it bothering you?" Les reiterated.

"Does it bother me that my ex-live-in lover, who was a card carrying gold digger, trapped some other poor schmuck into bankrolling her? I wish him luck." Patrick sighed, disgusted with himself for barking at Les. "I'm sorry. I didn't mean to bite your head off."

"Hey, we've been friends long enough for me to take a little heat. Still mad as hell, I take it?"

"Only at myself when I think of how close I came to believing her."

"You didn't come too close. Before you popped the question you had the good sense to have her background and history checked into."

"Not something I'm proud of," Patrick murmured.

"It isn't a crime for someone in your position to protect himself. What else should you have done after hearing that rumor about her? What I want to know is how you *feel* about her getting married."

"Glad it wasn't me," he answered without having to think about it because it was true. "And cautious," he added, no less certain even though it came as an after-thought.

"You could save yourself the worry by fraternizing only with heiresses who have enough of their own dough not to care about yours."

Patrick grimaced, picturing the women he knew who qualified. Pedigrees and country clubs and social status were more important than flesh-and-blood people to them. Then, suddenly, he had an image of Mitch Cuddy in her jeans and T-shirt, driving her old pink hearse and taking care of her slightly batty grandmother. It made him smile. "No, thanks. Heiresses may have enough gold not to dig for someone else's, but money tends to be too important to them, too. To the ones I've met anyway."

"I guess you're just going to have to do something out of an old movie—you know, mix among the common folk like you're one of them and hide the fact that you're a big bucks magazine mogul until after you've met one who loves you only for your sterling character.''

''Right. But for now I think I'll just concentrate on *Probe*.''

''Back to that again, huh? And just when I was trying so hard to keep your mind off of it. How about if we delay the premier issue again and wait until Amy divorces her oil tycoon and takes him for half of everything he owns. We could do a piece on how the unsuspecting rich get swindled out of their hard-earned money in the name of love—there's an injustice for you.''

Patrick laughed wryly at that. ''Two problems. One is that we can't wait that long, and two, we're out for the underdog, remember? If she takes five of his ten billion I don't think the guy is going to starve. We need to do some good here, L.B.''

''I take it you haven't come up with a launch angle, either.''

''The most interesting thing I've run into is a UFO reported by Al's house-sitter.''

''A UFO reported by Al's house-sitter,'' Les repeated sarcastically. ''Since when would old Al, who trusts everybody, hire somebody to sit his house while he's gone?''

''If the rhapsody in his voice when I talked to him on the phone last night is any indication, I'd say since he met Hilly Nolan six months ago. She and her granddaughter are staying there while he's off in a golf tournament.''

''And one of them is a nut who sees UFOs?''

Patrick took a drink of his coffee. For some reason it was all right for him to think of Hilly as batty, but not for Les to call her a nut. "I don't think either one of them is a nut. Hilly's just an old dear who had a scare."

"Why do you sound defensive?"

"Did I? No reason. I just like them."

"Them?"

"Yes, them. Hilly is quite a character and her grand-daughter is, well, she's interesting. I don't know many people who drive a pink hearse. She has striking, curly red hair and the biggest, blackest eyes—"

"Doing a little rhapsodizing yourself, aren't you, Patrick?"

"Not until she starts calling me PD."

"Give me a break."

"When you give me a terrific lead article to launch this magazine. That, my friend, is the most important thing in my life right now."

"If we don't count redheads with the biggest, blackest eyes you've ever seen," Les jabbed again.

Patrick ignored it. "I just wanted to let you know I was home. Call me if anything comes up."

"You got it."

Patrick took the phone back to the counter, refilled his cup and then sat at the table again. He riffled through the papers in his briefcase, sorting them into piles. But his mind was not on work. It was still on Mitch Cuddy. It had been on Mitch Cuddy well into the previous night when he should have been sleeping. There was something about her...

Maybe it was her standoffishness, he thought wryly. After the tenacious pursuit of Amy Rogers and what that had led to, maybe a woman who only seemed to want to get rid of him was attractive.

He discarded the idea. He hadn't turned neurotic. But he had sworn to take a long time out from women and he had meant it. Yet there was something intriguing about Mitch that he couldn't seem to resist. Some pull that had made him follow her all the way up to Al's house last night with his eyes trained on that tight little backside of hers when he should have been rushing to see if Al needed him.

For a moment he was lost in that image again, as surely as if she were standing in front of him. Then he shook his head to clear it. "A story, Drake. You need to find a story."

He picked up a list of ideas one of Probe's reporters had submitted, and tried to read it. But he couldn't concentrate. His mind kept wandering to UFOs and old Al having a romance and red, curly hair and black eyes and . . .

Patrick shook the image out of his thoughts, and went for more coffee. Through the window over his sink the glimmer of the pool caught his eye. It had just been cleaned and filled the day before—the bill had been in his mailbox when he got home last night. That meant the water would still be pretty cold.

He set his cup down and went out onto the bricked patio. Crossing to the pool he stuck his foot in the water. It wasn't icy but it was a long way from warm, so he dived in. In lieu of a cold shower.

After a restless night, Mitch woke up at seven-ten on Saturday morning. She groaned when she realized how early it was and rolled over to try to go back to sleep.

Why was the house so quiet? she wondered. Hilly was an early riser and believing that it was a healthy practice, she usually put every effort into making noise so Mitch would get up. The older woman must have gone out for a walk the way she sometimes did first thing in the morning, Mitch thought, and told herself to take what she could get and go back to sleep.

She tried. But she couldn't. She'd gone to bed with the image of Patrick Drake in her head and there he was again, keeping her awake just the same.

Nuts. It really was just plain crazy. She was a thirty-three-year-old woman with her life set on a course she had chosen, a course that could not, under any circumstances, involve a man and a romance.

A man and a romance? That was quite a leap from just meeting the next-door neighbor and having a drink with him. Ridiculous.

Mitch flung the sheets away and sat up on the edge of the bed.

It was Hilly's fault, she decided. Hilly was so caught up in her own romantic whirl that it was rubbing off. But one of them had to stay sane. And it had better be Mitch.

She gathered a long, heavy mass of her hair into a ponytail and went to get a rubber band. Like all of Alfred's house, this room was very formal. The bed had four posters so high they nearly touched the ceiling, an armoire encased a color television, and Mitch's chin barely topped the highboy mahogany dresser that stood between two long, thin windows.

Her rubber band was on a silver salver. Once she had wrapped it around her hair she stepped to the left window and opened the maroon velvet drapes. Because Patrick Drake's house was situated on the curve in the street, his backyard faced the side of Alfred's house. And the first thing Mitch's gaze fell on when those drapes were opened was the man himself diving into his pool directly below her bedroom window.

She hadn't realized before just how close a view she had of his backyard. For a moment she stood there staring. So what if he's swimming? she asked herself. So what if his body was a rippling streak under the surface of the water? Go take a bath the way you intended to.

Steadfastly Mitch rounded the bureau to open the rest of the drapes. Don't look, she commanded herself. But she did anyway.

He had surfaced to do a backstroke. Long, muscular arms came up out of the water on either side of an angular face. It seemed even sharper with his hair slicked back away from it. His eyes were closed, his chin a shade darker with a night's growth of beard. His neck was thick and powerful looking though not disproportionately large. His tan skin glistened where the early-morning sun touched him. Dark hair lightly shadowed the wide span of his chest, and Mitch's gaze followed it where it became a single, narrow line that ended at his navel, the center of a narrow, flat stomach. He wasn't wearing swimming trunks, but instead had on yellow shorts, soaked clear through and clinging to...

Mitch caught her breath and jerked her gaze up to the single cloud that drifted in the sky. This was like reverse peeping. Instead of looking in someone's window she was looking out of hers, over an eight-foot hedge he probably thought gave him privacy.

Go on, go take your bath, she ordered yet again. But on their own her eyes stole another look.

He was just hoisting himself out of the pool. She watched the flex of the muscles in his back. She stared at the vision of his tight derriere through the nearly transparent shorts. He rose all the way out of the water and those thick, hairy thighs, bulging calves and bare feet came into view. She swallowed with difficulty as her gaze went up to watch him smooth his wet hair back with both hands. Then he clasped them at his nape and spread his arms in a stretch that made a crease down his spine.

Incredible. Magnificent. Man.

Then all of a sudden he hooked his thumbs in the waistband of his shorts and slipped them down, unknowingly exposing his glorious, bare backside to her.

Mitch jumped back, flattening herself against the side of the dresser as if she had been spotted. Holding her neck stiff she stared up at the ceiling. Her heart was pounding and it was nearly impossible to breathe.

*Low, Mitch. You've really sunk to the depths.*

But as if pulled by a string attached to her nose, her head turned to the window again. From that single cloud in the sky her gaze dipped to the thatched rooftop of Patrick's house.

Peeping Tom, she called herself.

Her gaze slid to the eaves.

Voyeur.

She saw the twin Victorian street lamps on either side of the short wall that bordered the patio.

Peeker.

There it was again. The pool. Clear blue water as smooth as glass. Wet footprints darkening the patio bricks in a path to the house. Those yellow shorts were draped along the back of a lounge chair. But Patrick was nowhere in sight.

Mitch breathed a sigh of relief. Good. She was glad he'd gone in. Glad to be saved from herself.

And disappointed.

After her bath Mitch dressed in a pair of lightweight white cotton pants and a pink T-shirt, cuffing the sleeves and knotting one corner of the hem at her hip. Leaving her hair in the ponytail, and her feet bare she went downstairs, arriving at the foyer at the same moment Hilly came in the front door.

"Good morning, good morning, good morning," the older woman trilled. A headband circled her brow and left her snowy curls popping out all over. She wore a tank top, running shorts and tennis shoes that accentuated her birdlike legs.

"I thought you'd probably gone out for a walk," Mitch said as she led the way into the kitchen where Hilly perched on a bar stool at the end of the counter that divided the cooking space from a breakfast nook. Mitch opened the refrigerator. "Iced tea?" she asked, holding the pitcher up.

"Oh, please. It's another scorcher out there."

Mitch filled two glasses and brought them to the counter where Hilly handed her a bran muffin from a plate. "I made these this morning before I left. They're still warm."

Mitch thanked her and took a bite while Hilly grabbed a muffin for herself.

"So," Mitch began. "What happened last night, Hil?"

Hilly rolled her eyes and shook her head. "What a mess, wasn't it? Police and paramedics. Bunch of panic pushers."

"But what happened?"

"I was reading the *Wall Street Journal* and thinking that we should go for ice cream when you got home. I thought I heard a noise outside the window in the living room. At first I just figured it was a cat but then, out of the corner of my eye, I thought I saw someone crouching in the bushes out there."

"Oh, no, here we go again," Mitch sighed, losing her appetite for the muffin.

"I know," Hilly agreed and then went on. "That's what I thought, too. Right away I pulled all the drapes and then I called security. It didn't even occur to me that they'd call the police. I thought they would handle it themselves and just scare off whoever it was, if it was anyone at all. But before I knew what was happening I was surrounded by uniforms and white coats. When they didn't find a sign of anyone or anything outside they started asking if there was some reason for me to be so jumpy. Well, of course I couldn't tell them the truth." Hilly's tone turned curt. "I had overheard one officer make a snide remark about how the old bag— meaning me—probably thought she'd seen a UFO. I just decided on the spot: why not. You want a crazy old lady, I'll give you a crazy old lady." She shrugged, throwing both of her hands in the air as if in surrender. "So I took it from there."

"You know that this is just the sort of thing that got you into trouble," Mitch reminded her.

Pulling her headband off and shaking her hair loose, Hilly was obviously unperturbed by Mitch's concern. "Should I have told them the truth?" she challenged.

They both knew the answer to that, so instead Mitch asked, "Did you get a glimpse of who was in the bushes?"

Hilly shook her head. "No. I pulled those drapes so fast it would have made your head spin. Thought it was more important to keep whoever it was from getting a glimpse of me than for me to see him—if it really was a person."

Mitch sipped her tea for a moment before broaching the subject she knew Hilly was not going to like.

"Maybe we should start thinking about leaving Colorado."

"I knew you were going to say that, Mitchy."

"And I knew you weren't going to want to do it."

"I just don't think we have to. At least not yet. I barely saw a moving shadow out of the corner of my eye. It could have been a cat or a dog the way the police said. I went out the minute it was light this morning and couldn't find any footprints in the dirt around the bushes."

Mitch played devil's advocate. "There's more grass around the bushes than there is dirt, and there wouldn't be any footprints left in that."

Hilly looked her straight in the eye. "I don't think there's anything to worry about. Not yet, anyway. I really care for Alfred, Mitchy. The way I cared for Mike, the way I didn't think I'd ever feel for any man again after he died. I'd like to enjoy that for a while."

"We've made it this far by not taking any chances, by always playing it safe, Hil."

"I know, but we've never run from shadows, either. If I really thought what I saw last night was something other than an animal I'd say load up the clock and let's go. But I just don't think that's necessary."

"Would you if it weren't for Alfred?"

Hilly shrugged.

"Don't you think that the longer you indulge in this fling the harder it will be to leave him?" Mitch said.

"Maybe so," Hilly admitted.

But suddenly Mitch saw the other side of this, too. How much of her own disquiet was influencing her urge to move on? She'd had that odd feeling on the way home last night, but that was not enough reason to refuse Hilly a little romance that could well be the last she ever had. It wasn't fair to pull Hilly away from Alfred just because Mitch was having some trouble keeping her own juices from stirring at the thought of Patrick Drake.

"No, I don't suppose we need to go now. But we do need to keep our eyes and ears open."

"Sure, sure," Hilly agreed as if it didn't need to be said.

"And another thing. We had better avoid Patrick Drake like the plague. The last thing we need is to get chummy with some nosy ex-newspaper reporter."

As if on cue, the man in question appeared at the sliding glass back door and knocked.

"Speak of the devil," Hilly said gaily, motioning him to come in.

He slid the door open and stepped into the kitchen, answering Hilly's good-morning. "I don't ordinarily go visiting this early but I saw you out walking, Hilly, and since I'm extending this invitation at the last minute, I decided it didn't need to be any later than it already was."

"Iced tea?" Hilly offered.

"No, thanks. I only have a minute."

Mitch was having difficulty joining in their easy repartee. As if she had X-ray vision she was seeing Patrick the way he'd been an hour before rather than dressed in navy-blue shorts and a white T-shirt as he was now. She tried hard to concentrate on what he was saying.

"I just wondered if the two of you would come for dinner tonight? I don't get the chance to cook too often—when you're alone it isn't much fun. So would you join me?"

"Isn't that nice," Hilly said before Mitch could open her mouth. "We'd love it. Wouldn't we, Mitchy?"

Mitch stared daggers at the older woman. But what else could she say? She tried, "You don't have to do that. After just getting home from a long time away, you must have a million things to do without cooking on top of it."

He looked directly into her eyes and smiled slowly. "Believe it or not, with the exception of some paperwork I don't have anything else to do. And even if I did, cooking for the two of you would still be preferable." His tone dropped an octave and sounded more intimate, as if he was speaking to Mitch alone. "How about it? I really want to spend the evening with you...both."

Now there definitely wasn't anything else she could say. Mitch tried to smile but her cheeks quivered with the effort. "Well...I...that would be nice. Thank you."

"Great," he said only to her.

"Wonderful," Hilly broke in gleefully. "We make a black-bottom rum pie that's to die for. How about if we bring it as our contribution?"

Patrick was slow to break the hold his eyes had on Mitch's. But he finally did, looking at the older woman. "How did you know I'm crazy for black-bottom rum pie?"

Hilly laughed. "It's written all over you. What time?"

"I'll come through the gate in the hedge the way I did just now and walk you over about seven."

"You don't have to do that," Mitch said quickly.

"I want to." That seemed to finish it. "I take it the rest of last night was all right? No more disturbances, alien or otherwise?"

"I slept like a baby," Hilly assured him.

"Mitch?" There was a warm familiarity in his tone that strummed a chord in her.

"No problem," she clipped out.

"Good. Then I'll be back here at your kitchen door at seven."

He was gone as quickly as he had appeared and before Mitch could say anything to Hilly the elderly woman hopped down from her stool and said, "I really need a shower," as she jogged out of the room.

Mitch refused to change her clothes for the occasion of Patrick's dinner, which she also refused to consider an occasion. What she did do, though, was to loosely knot her hair and convince herself that it was only for the sake of coolness.

As she let Patrick in the back door she tried not to notice how nice he looked in silver-gray corduroy shorts and an ice-blue polo shirt that brought out the color of his eyes. He smelled of that clean, spicy after-shave again and the impact it all had on her was much stronger than she liked.

"I'll call Hilly," she told him, leaving him standing in the middle of the kitchen while she went to the foot of the stairs and tried to regain control of herself.

But her escape was foiled when Patrick followed her. "Don't rush her if she isn't ready. We can wait," he said in a tone of voice that fired up Mitch's senses.

Just then Hilly appeared at the top of the stairs, dressed in her bathrobe, holding a washcloth to her brow. Mitch knew instantly what the older woman was up to, and wanted to scream.

"I don't think I can make it," Hilly sighed convincingly as she held on to the banister with her free hand

and descended slowly, theatrically. "I have a migraine headache."

Hilly never got headaches, migraines or otherwise. But of course Patrick didn't know that, and if he saw through her playacting he didn't show it. "Have you taken anything for it?" he asked, concern deepening his voice and drawing his eyebrows close together.

"I have special medicine that I just took. It puts me to sleep and then when I wake up the pain is gone." She stopped on the bottom step, holding the newel post for support.

Mitch turned to Patrick. "I'm sorry. I hope you didn't go to too much trouble. You'll just have to give us a rain check."

"Oh, no, Mitchy." Hilly was obviously ready for her. "You go on with Patrick. I'm headed right to bed for the night. It would be silly for you to stay here while I sleep. You know how these headaches are, and there's nothing in the world you can do. Honestly. I want you and Patrick to enjoy yourselves without me. I would only feel worse thinking I had ruined everyone's evening." The older woman looked at Patrick. "Now promise me you won't let her stay here. She worries about me, but tonight there's no cause. So take her next door and feed her a good meal while I go back upstairs."

Hilly didn't wait for an answer, or for Mitch to say anything else. Instead she turned and went the way she'd come.

"You're sure you'll be all right here alone, Hilly?" Patrick asked her back.

Hilly kept on climbing, lifting her hand off the banister long enough to flap her hand. "Positive. Have a lovely time. I'll call you both if I need anything."

Patrick faced Mitch. "Why don't I bring everything over here? It doesn't matter where we eat and then you'll be able to check on her."

Mitch thought about that for a moment. It would serve Hilly right. If she and Patrick stayed here Hilly would have to spend the whole night playing sick in her bedroom. But in the end Mitch couldn't do it to her. It would mean Hilly would miss dinner and Mitch worried too much about the older woman's real health to chance anything.

"No, that's too much bother. Hilly's right, she doesn't need me here while she sleeps."

"You're sure."

"I'm sure." Besides, it also gave her a good excuse to end the evening early, something she couldn't control if he was here.

"Shall we go then?"

Mitch took the pie she and Hilly had made that afternoon, handing it to Patrick while she locked the sliding door after them. They circled Alfred's pool to the cobbled path that led to a heavy, wooden, English garden gate built into an arch in the hedge. She opened it but he waited for her to go through first. And then there she was, face-to-face with his swimming pool, shaded now that the sun was low enough to be blocked by the house. Mitch fought against the memory of all she had seen there that morning but lost the battle for a few moments.

The sound of the hedge gate closing brought her out of her reverie and Mitch made a beeline around the pool to Patrick's house, pretending to brush something off her white pants.

"I did things pretty casually," he told her as he let her into the kitchen through French doors.

"Good. I'm not a fancy person."

His kitchen was more warm and homey than Alfred's, Mitch thought as she glanced around. The walls were redbrick, which gave the area a charming country flavor and made the lack of decorative knickknacks less noticeable.

"I thought we'd have a glass of wine while I put the last touch on the snapper," he said as he set the pie in the refrigerator. He poured the wine that had already been opened. "I thought about putting three thick filets on the barbecue but I'm trying to avoid temptation and eat less red meat."

Mitch accepted the wine, wondering at the sensation when her fingers brushed his. It was as if a faint electrical charge had shot up her arm. "Hilly would have applauded you for resisting. She's a health nut."

Patrick smiled up at her for a second before taking a poaching pan out of the oven and reaching for a jar of paprika. "I guessed as much. I saw her out walking at quite a clip this morning. What did her headband say? I could only make out wild."

"Born To Be Wild," Mitch supplied, smiling in response to the statement as well as the grin that erupted on Patrick's face. She liked the way the lines fanned around his eyes. In repose he looked serious and yet when those creases formed he seemed lighthearted and far more carefree. "Is there something I can do to help?" she asked, dragging her glance away.

He lifted the fish out onto a platter with a flourish. "Grab whatever you can carry and take it to the table so we can eat."

Mitch took both her wineglass and his in one hand and the salad bowl in the other, and followed him around a butcher block into the eating space where an oak table was already set and waiting.

"Alfred didn't know Hilly when I left. How did they meet?" he asked as he lit a single candle in the center of the table.

The subject of the older woman was a comfortable one for Mitch; it helped to put her slightly at ease. "Well, Hilly has a theory," she told him as he went into the kitchen for a basket of dinner rolls and a bowl of brown rice. When he was back and sitting around the corner from her she went on. "She says that for a woman her age the obituaries are better than the personal ads for finding available men."

Patrick stopped in the middle of serving the fish to look at her. "This seems too obvious, but aren't all the men listed there dead?"

"What she does is look for funerals where there are a lot of survivors. She says the more people still alive, the bigger the funeral and the more likely she is to meet someone. Alfred was at the funeral of a friend's brother."

"And Hilly didn't know the deceased?"

"Or anyone else there when she went."

Patrick laughed. It was a nice sound, deep and rumbling, but more it held a warmth and genuine appreciation for Hilly without sounding as if he found the older woman deranged. It was an attitude Mitch was particularly vulnerable to.

"Doesn't she get depressed going to funerals?" he asked.

"Not Hilly. She says it's all part of the natural order of things."

"And what about you?" His tone of voice took on that vaguely intimate timbre for the second time.

Mitch swallowed a forkful of rice and nodded her head. "I suppose she's right. Death is all part of the natural order of things, but thinking about it reminds me how old she is and that bothers me."

"No." He only partially suppressed a laugh. "I meant do you go looking for available men at funerals, too?"

"Oh, no," Mitch blurted out. "I mean I don't ever go looking for available men."

"Do you prefer unavailable ones?" he teased.

"No." Again it came too quickly. "I don't prefer any... I mean I just don't have time for romance or relationships."

"What do you do?"

"You mean for a living?" One of the many dreaded questions. He nodded and Mitch stalled by sipping her wine, wiping her mouth, and pushing her dish away. "Until last night I was a telephone answering service operator."

"What are you today?" he asked as if he thought she was joking.

"Unemployed."

He seemed to realize suddenly that she wasn't kidding. "By choice?"

"It was a temporary job."

"Oh, I see. You haven't been in Colorado long enough to find something permanent. What are you looking for? Maybe I can help."

"I never really settled into any one career," she said reticently, feeling her way as she went. "I just do any odd jobs I can find to get us by."

He sat back in his chair and studied her openly. "That surprises me. You seem so serious and practical."

Not something she heard as a compliment. Mitch ran her fingertip around the rim of her wineglass, refusing to meet his eyes. When she answered him her voice was tight. "Yes, well, I guess between Hilly and me one of us has to be."

He leaned forward, closing his hand around hers. "Don't be offended. I didn't mean that as an insult. You have a quiet dignity that's very attractive. And I think it's terrific that Hilly's flamboyance doesn't threaten you. Another person—certainly a lot of women I know—would be vying with her for some of the attention her personality naturally attracts, but you don't do that. And rather than resent it, I have the feeling that you enjoy her. That kind of affection and loyalty are uncommon."

Mitch was trying hard to ignore the sparkling currents his hand around hers was generating, coupled with this open statement of his admiration. She could feel embarrassment coloring her cheeks. She was grateful that it had gotten dark enough so that the only light in the room was from the single candle. "I don't think I'm quite ready for sainthood," she said, laughing at herself. "It just never occurred to me to compete with Hilly. I owe her more than any person on earth."

"Why is that?"

The question was, why had Mitch said it? She never offered personal history information. But now that she had gotten herself in this far, she had to go the rest of the way. "Hilly took me in when I was twelve and my parents were both killed in a plane crash."

He still cupped her hand around the wineglass. His thumb ran up and down her index finger in a feathery stroke that made even more sparks dance up her arm.

"But as your grandmother that was more or less her duty, wasn't it?"

Mitch suddenly remembered the lies of last night that complicated her true admission. For a moment she silently fought to regain her aplomb. Then she said, "I guess I just never looked at it as something she had to do."

"You may not be ready for sainthood but I'm really impressed that you don't take for granted something most people would."

"I don't know about that," she said, buying herself some time to think of a way out of this intensely uncomfortable conversation.

He did it for her. "So why do you call your grandmother by her first name?"

Oh, boy. Back to the lies. "What do you call your grandmother?" She tried offense instead of defense. She glanced up and caught him smiling at her.

He squeezed her hand one last time and sat back again, twirling his glass. "I never knew either of them."

No help there. Mitch conceded and made up an answer. "Calling her anything else aged her too much."

"And why the different last names? Are you her married daughter's daughter or is there a husband somewhere in your past?"

Multiple choice lies. "I've never been married," she chose the truth and lied by default.

Mitch wondered what time it was and if she could leave now without being rude. It was bad enough to be so physically affected by him. Being interrogated by him only compounded things and he was shooting the questions at her so fast she couldn't break his stride long enough to ask any of her own the way Hilly had taught her to make polite conversation.

"Where do you live when you aren't house-sitting?" He shot another one.

"We don't have a place right now."

"But I thought you were visiting Hilly while she did the house-sitting?"

"You've found us out," she tried joking with him. "It's really Hilly and I who landed here last night in a spacecraft. We're the first wave of a full-scale invasion by alien life-forms. Change the concept of your magazine from righting injustices to proving UFOs are for real and you've got the story you're looking for to launch it."

He laughed that hearty laugh again and this time the electrical currents skittered through her without his even touching her. "Okay, okay, I get the picture. Hang up my nosy-neighbor hat. Add asking too many questions to the list of occupational hazards I fall into without thinking about it." His pale blue eyes stared into hers. "There is one thing I do know, though. You're a long way from an alien life-form."

"Don't be too sure. We eggplant people have the power to alter our appearance at will."

"Please don't. I like your appearance." He paused a beat and his expression confirmed it. Then he said, "I also like your sense of humor. I take it eggplant people is what Hilly thought she saw last night."

"Mmm." It was suddenly very tempting to stay and bask in the warmth of that appreciation. Too tempting. "I think I'd better get home and see how her headache is."

"But we haven't had your pie."

"Still, I don't want to leave her alone any longer."

He was up and pulling her chair out before she could do it herself. "I understand. Especially after last night. I'll walk you back."

The air outside was warm and still and resplendent with the mingled scents of greenery and flowers and clean pool water. Mitch breathed it in deeply to bolster her determination to resist the pull she felt toward this man. As she preceded him through the gate in the hedge she spoke in a light unaffected tone to hide the fact that her insides were roiling. "Thank you for dinner. You really are a good cook."

"Anytime."

As they skirted Alfred's pool Patrick took her elbow, though the tiled deck was dry and there was no need. Mitch vaguely considered pulling out of his grasp, but suddenly couldn't find the strength or the inclination.

A patio light burned by the back door and when Mitch held the ring of keys up to find the one she needed Patrick gently took them out of her hand and did it for her. But once the door was unlocked, rather than sliding it open, he turned to face her. For just a moment his eyes looked into hers and then he slowly leaned in to kiss her.

*Move away,* she told herself. But instead she tipped her chin slightly to accept his warm, slightly moist lips. It was the briefest of kisses, not intimate, not passionate, and yet it had the power to send shock waves rippling throughout her entire body. When he stepped back, there was a split second during which she wasn't sure if her knees would hold her.

He reached up to run the back of his fingers across her temple. "Good night, Mitch," he said softly, in a voice just raspy enough to leave her wondering if it was possible that he, too, had been as affected as she by such a simple kiss.

Before she remembered to answer him, he turned and she watched his back as he slipped through the gate. She swallowed and blinked. Then she slid the door open and went into the dark house.

"This can't happen," she said to herself once the door was closed.

"Of course it can," came Hilly's impish voice in the darkness. "It just did."

## Chapter Three

As Mitch came downstairs on Sunday morning the smell of garlic permeated the air and the rhythmic counting of Jack LaLanne's exercise tape greeted her. The sound and scent brought an instant flashback to the days of her adolescence with Hilly. Only then Jack LaLanne—Hilly's fitness guru and secret heartthrob— had come over the television on his own daily program. Breakfast, she knew by the smell, would be Hilly's favorite—carrot juice and hot cereal cooked with a clove of garlic.

At the foot of the stairs, Mitch paused to look into Alfred's book-lined den. Hilly's back was to her. She was holding on to a chair and kicking her leg out to the side just the way Jack LaLanne did on the TV screen directly in front of her.

Mitch smiled at the familiar sight.

*"Get the chair, Mitchy,"* she remembered Hilly telling her every weekday morning for so many years. Mitch always did, dragging a ladder-back chair to the front of the television while Hilly brought out the elasticized chest pull and the jump rope.

*"Look at the body on that man,"* Hilly would say at least once a week. *"Just like a young Adonis. Who would ever guess how old he is? It must all work to keep him in that shape."* And then she would follow along with the same vigor she did now, talking back to everything he said as if he were in the room with her.

The old memory tightened Mitch's throat. There was no one in the world like Hilly. And no one Mitch had ever loved more.

*Where would I be without you?*

Used, abused and exploited, was the answer. Had Hilly not fought for guardianship and custody of her, Mitch would have been sent to her mother's cousin Bill and his harridan wife, Susan. Cousin Bill, who Mitch had learned at the onset of puberty to avoid rather than be pulled onto his lap for one of his seemingly innocent bear hugs that always camouflaged his hands on her young breasts and his knee up between her legs. And his wife, Susan, who wanted her own personal servant in the form of the twelve-year-old Mitch.

Instead, she had had Hilly. Wonderfully eccentric, full-of-life Hilly, who had taken Mitch into her home and into her heart simultaneously and turned what had suddenly become a child's worst nightmare into a whole new world.

*Death comes in threes,* Mitch remembered her saying. *My Mike last month and your momma and daddy now. But you and I, Mitchy, we'll have each other. I'll see to that, no matter what it takes. And we'll go on.*

And they had. With gusto and verve, the way Hilly did everything.

As Mitch stood there watching and remembering the tape ended and Hilly kissed the tips of her fingers to Jack LaLanne. Then she jogged over to the video machine and turned it and the television off. "Oh, good morning, Mitchy," she said enthusiastically when she swiveled around and saw her at the doorway. "Did you get to wake up to the sound of Jack's voice? Now there's a way to start the day." Hilly wore only her tennis shoes and an extralarge man's white undershirt that came to her knobby knees.

"I've always said that," Mitch laughed. "Those new alarm clocks that talk should have Jack LaLanne's voice programmed into them."

Hilly flipped her index finger in Mitch's direction. "Now there's an idea. Maybe we should write someone and suggest it." Then the older woman headed for the kitchen. "Come on, I have our week-starter breakfast waiting. Only I made your hot cereal without the garlic so you won't have polluted breath," she added slyly, throwing Mitch a look out of the corner of her eye.

When Mitch had come in the night before she had dodged Hilly's questions about her dinner with Patrick. She knew she wasn't going to get away with it much longer, but she decided to be obtuse to Hilly's pointed comment. "It's about time. You know I hate hot cereal with garlic and you still make me eat a spoonful of it every Sunday morning."

"Good for you. I read an article about a man who lived to be a hundred and sixteen because he ate garlic every day."

"Not in his breakfast cereal, I'll bet," Mitch answered as she always did when Hilly told her this.

"Well, I just thought that for this once you could do without the garlic in favor of—" Hilly raised her bushy eyebrows and grinned lasciviously "—affairs of the heart."

"In that case I could eat the garlic."

Mitch put ice in her carrot juice, knowing it was futile and nothing made it any more palatable, and joined Hilly in the boothed breakfast nook where the older woman had brought two bowls of the hot cereal.

"So tell me all about it," Hilly demanded outright.

"He made red snapper, rice and salad. We had wine with dinner. I left before we cut the pie and he could ask me any more probing questions."

"How probing?" Again Hilly used a suggestive tone of voice.

"You have a dirty mind for a nice, little old lady, do you know that?"

"Yep."

"Well, most of his questions were about you as my grandmother. I think maybe he has a crush on you."

"Hmph. Wasn't me he was locking lips with under the moon last night."

Mitch drank the entire glass of carrot juice before she gagged on it, and followed it down with a bite of jellied toast. "Would you believe I had something in my eye and he was trying to get it out?"

"There weren't any eyes open."

"Were you watching through binoculars?"

"Didn't need to. This carrot juice keeps my eyes working fine."

Mitch took a deep breath and sighed. "It was just a mistake, Hil. Maybe I'd had too much of his wine. He really is someone to stay clear of. He asks enough questions to head a senate investigation committee. So stop your matchmaking before it gets us into a jam we can't get out of."

Hilly scoffed that away with the wave of her hand. "Don't give me that too much wine business. You like that man."

"That isn't the point." She wished it wasn't true, but she did like Patrick Drake.

"The point is that you should go for it," Hilly said, jabbing the air with her thumb for emphasis.

"That would be playing with fire." In more ways than one.

Hilly ate a few spoonfuls of her garlic hot cereal. When she spoke again there was compassion—and no teasing—in her tone of voice. "You came to me a serious child, Mitchy. I tried to lighten that up and for a while I succeeded. Now it's my fault that you're back to being serious. I just want to see it let up again."

Mitch's throat tightened once more. She reached for Hilly's hand and squeezed it hard, all the while looking her straight in the eye. "None of this is your fault and I don't ever want to hear you say it is." Then she smiled. "And that's the second time in less than twelve hours that I've been called serious. I don't think I like it."

Hilly was back to her old self. "Good!" she proclaimed. "Then indulge in a little romance. We've both earned it."

Mitch gave a mock shriek.

Hilly ignored it. "I have a sixth sense about our Mr. Patrick Drake, Mitchy. He's a good one, I can just tell. And even from the little Alfred has said about him, it's obvious he has integrity. I think we can trust him in spite of his profession." She hunched her shoulders and poked her head out the way she had done when Mitch was a child and she was trying to entice her into trying something new. "Come on. Have a fling."

It was tempting, there was no doubt about that. The chemistry was there—that kiss the previous night had only illustrated it all the more.

"Let your hair down a little," Hilly went on, pulling a strand from Mitch's ponytail.

"There's too much at stake," she said, her puny tone an echo of her weakening resolve.

"We don't have to let him know anything we don't want him to know. Besides, who says you have to talk? Just keep him occupied. Looked to me like that wouldn't be too hard to do."

Mitch thought about that kiss again. Actually, since it had happened, she had found it difficult not to think about it. But she shook her head. "It just isn't smart, Hil. And I don't want us both leaving here with broken hearts when the time comes to move on. If you want to put yours on the line that's up to you, but I don't want any part of it."

Mitch and Hilly spent the morning companionably poring over the Sunday newspapers, ending with Hilly reading the comic strips while Mitch went through the want ads in search of jobs. Hilly decided to bend a little on her health regime to have a chili cheese dog for lunch. Then they did some grocery shopping and went to the video store to rent movies for the evening.

While Hilly cooked dinner Mitch indulged herself in the second bath of the day, lounging for a while in tepid, perfumed water to wash away the sticky feeling left from being out in the nearly hundred-degree heat.

The specially blended bath oil had been a Christmas gift from Hilly and Mitch had sprinkled it liberally into the tub as it filled. The water felt silky and sensuous and for some reason that made her think about Patrick in spite of all of her resolves not to.

After her bath she put on a pair of lightweight jeans and a pale cream-colored V-neck T-shirt. For no particular reason except that she felt like it, she added just a touch of peach eye shadow to her usual faint liner and mascara, and dusted slightly more blush across her cheekbones. She brushed her hair out and, in deference to the heat that penetrated even the air-conditioned house, swept it back with a comb that left a cascade of curls hanging down the back of her head. She finished with just a dab of perfume, then headed downstairs.

She made it to the swinging door that connected the foyer to the kitchen before she heard Hilly say, "It's sort of dandelion soup. Very good for you. I make it with dandelions, a little pork, a little tomato, beaten eggs and Romano cheese. You have to eat with us to see how good it is. And afterward you can stay and watch the movies we rented. We'll make an evening of it."

Mitch rolled her eyes. She didn't have to see to know it was Patrick whom the older woman was inviting to dinner. The sensible side of Mitch railed against it almost loudly enough to drown out the tiny part of her that was glad to spend more time with the neighbor.

She pushed through the door and there he was, slicing a crusty loaf of Italian bread. He wore khaki shorts and a red mock-turtleneck T-shirt, the long sleeves pushed to his elbows. He looked the way she felt, as if he had just stepped out of a shower, and she reluctantly admitted to herself that the sight of him stirred her. Quickly Mitch glanced away, wishing for imperviousness.

"Here she is," Hilly announced. "Patrick came to talk to you about something and he's staying for dinner and our film fest."

"Uh-huh," Mitch said noncommittally. "He probably thinks we're crazy to be eating weeds."

Patrick chuckled. "It is a little strange, I'll admit. But it smells delicious."

"It really is good," Mitch admitted. "One of my favorites. We picked the dandelions in the spring and Hilly froze what we didn't eat then."

His eyes caught hers. There was an intriguing sparkle in them. "And do you mind sharing?"

"There's plenty," Hilly put in as she stirred the steaming pot.

He was a tall, muscular, freshly scrubbed male beauty. And he was their guest for the evening. There was nothing she could do about it but resign herself. Mitch took a deep breath and graciously said, "No, I don't mind sharing. I'll set the table." Then she added as an afterthought, "But I'm warning you that Hilly picked out the movies. They could be anything from cartoons to the goriest thriller ever made. You're taking your chances twice tonight."

He smiled at her, a wide, warm, appreciative grin. "I'm a gambling man. I'll risk it."

"So what did you want to talk to Mitch about?" Hilly asked bluntly as they sat down to eat.

Patrick eyed his bowl dubiously and then seemed grateful to answer the question rather than taste this dandelion approximation of egg-drop soup. "I came to offer you a job," he said to Mitch. "I think tomorrow morning, with a little girl-Friday help, I can organize the stacks of papers I have at home. Then we could go in to the office in the afternoon and do the same thing there.

My secretary is swamped with her own work and this is stuff I've just been too busy to keep up with. It's mostly sorting and filing, but there's some work on the computer, too."

Before Mitch could say a word Hilly jumped in. "Oh, Mitch can do anything. She has a master's degree in business and marketing and she's a whiz with computers. She could reorganize your whole company if that's what you need. She's done it before."

Mitch cleared her throat. "Hilly," she drew the name out into several syllables. The older woman always got carried away with pride in Mitch and forgot that she shouldn't say so much—to this man in particular.

Mitch could feel Patrick watching her closely. "That's very interesting," he said, obviously meaning it. "I don't need the whole company reorganized, though. That's one of my long suits, too, something I usually end up doing when I get myself into a new venture. But I could certainly use the help tomorrow. How about it?"

Again it was Hilly who answered before Mitch could. "That would be wonderful. Why, just this morning she said there wasn't a single thing in the ads and she was going to have to tack up signs for odd jobs."

"I thought you needed me to take you to the vitamin store," Mitch put in pointedly to the older woman.

"That can wait until Tuesday."

"Then are we on for tomorrow?" Patrick asked.

For a moment Mitch stared at Hilly. But then she shrugged and gave in. "It would seem so."

"Wonderful," Hilly said. "Now quit stalling and taste the dandelions, Patrick."

It was Hilly who kept up most of the conversation through the meal that Patrick pronounced one of the best he had ever eaten. She expounded on the virtues of dandelions—high in iron and fiber—and gave him the history of their use in wine, vinegar and salads. Then she explained when the best time to pick them was, where and what to look for.

All the while Mitch surreptitiously watched Patrick's response to the older woman. He seemed to enjoy her dissertation, asking questions and prolonging a conversation that someone else might have tried to change. He teased and flattered Hilly, but never did he condescend to her or not take her seriously, or make fun of her in any way.

It made things more difficult for Mitch.

She wanted not to like him. Physical attraction was one thing. It might make it difficult to sleep alone at night, but it was somewhat easier to live with. Liking the man himself, finding his treatment of the single most important person in her life endearing, deepened the attraction. And an attraction that wasn't strictly physical and shallow was harder to suppress.

Kitchen cleanup, shared by the three of them, was quick and easy, though Hilly lamented how awful it was to wash dandelions. Then they settled in Alfred's den to watch movies. There were only two choices for seating—an overstuffed chair and a small love seat. Of course Hilly immediately took the single chair, leaving the cushioned love seat to Mitch and Patrick. Then she turned off the floorlamp, leaving the room lit only by the color picture on the television.

No points for subtlety, Hil, Mitch thought as she started the tape. Thwarting the older woman's machinations, Mitch sat on the floor with only her back against the love seat, as far away from Patrick as she could get.

Mitch had never heard of the two movies Hilly had chosen and within fifteen minutes after the first one began she realized why. *I should have known better.*

A scantily clad, very voluptuous woman was watching her daughter's boyfriend in their backyard swimming pool. The Fates and Hilly conspire, Mitch thought. There was too much similarity between what the camera focused on and what Mitch had seen of Patrick the morning before. And then it got worse as the woman took it a step beyond and seduced the beautifully well-built man.

Mitch wondered frantically how to escape. She fabricated an intense interest in the popcorn Hilly had made before they'd begun the movie. She sat up straighter and pulled her knees closer to her chest as if making herself comfortable, and willed the phone to ring so she could use that as an excuse to leave. It didn't.

Rather than watch the heightening sex scene on the screen she stared at the VCR on the shelf below the television, wishing the tape would break. But instead it was the woman's bra strap that snapped.

Why wouldn't the house catch fire when you wanted it to? Surely what was going on on that film was hot enough to ignite it. Prude, she accused, trying to shame herself into watching. But at just that moment the man in the movie stood with his back to the camera and peeled off his swimming trunks.

That was all she could take. Prude or not, Mitch quietly stood and left the den. Once outside she nearly ran for the back door, not stopping until she was on the patio. She took a deep breath and blew it out as if she were extinguishing flames, and stepped up onto the bench to sit on the picnic table.

"It's not cool enough out here to counteract the effects of that movie." Patrick's voice came from the sliding glass door only moments later, his teasing tone full of amusement.

"Would you believe I've already seen it?" she tried feebly.

"I don't think that particular film has been at a theater near you or anyone else."

He was silhouetted in the dim light, and Mitch hoped her features—particularly the blush she felt heating her cheeks—were as indiscernible as his. Then he stepped outside, closed the door behind him and sat on the table beside her, leaning back on his hands.

"You said yourself that since Hilly picked the movies they could be just about anything," he reminded her.

"I just didn't think they would be... so explicit."

"Actually I'm glad it turned out this way. It gives me a chance to be alone with you for a while."

"What time do you want me for work tomorrow?" she said, changing the subject rather than commenting on his admission.

"Is nine too early?"

"You're the boss."

"And that means you'll do anything I say?" he asked with obvious relish.

"Within reason." Mitch couldn't suppress a small smile. He was just so hard not to like.

"Guess that blows my ulterior motives."

She cast him a sidelong glance. "Do you have ulterior motives?" she asked, thinking about more than their wordplay.

"Could be." But he didn't expound. Instead he said, "So. I'm curious about your advanced degree, your computer wizardry and your organizational skills."

"You can't do the job interview after you've hired someone. It's before or never," she countered easily enough. The night was warm and peaceful and the darkness helped relax her.

"It's not an interview, just curiosity. I thought you said you had never settled into any one career."

"I've done a little of everything," she hedged.

"Where?"

"Adrift in the corporate world," she answered enigmatically. "Are you playing nosy neighbor again?"

"No, I just thought that with that education and those skills if you told me what you did or want to do I might be able to put you to work permanently for *Probe*."

Wouldn't that be dandy? Mitch thought. A job right in the midst of something that could ultimately do her damage, complete with a formal application, a social security number, withholding taxes, all those nifty little traceable legalities she avoided with informal jobs that usually paid her cash. "No, thanks. Hilly and I don't stay in one place long enough for anything like that."

"Why not?"

"We just need the freedom to move when the whim strikes."

"What are you, gypsies?" he teased in that deep, rich voice.

"Who else do you know would eat dandelions?" she countered with as much insincerity in her tone. "But I think free spirits sounds better."

"I seem to keep getting wrong impressions about you. I thought you had come to Colorado to live permanently. But now you tell me you move when the whim strikes. Is that seriously the way you live?"

"Pretty much."

"Have you always done that?"

"No. Only for about the last three years or so."

"Why did you start?"

The question was, why was she telling so much? She was getting as bad as Hilly. Mitch seized a scenario that she had used before, part truth and part not. "I had a good income from a job that I thought was absolutely secure. Then I found out that nothing really is. So Hilly and I took to the road to live an unencumbered life. At least with temporary jobs I know there's an end and when it's coming. I don't have high hopes and big plans for the future pinned on it so I'm never disappointed. And when the time comes, we just pack up the clock and leave. Two free spirits."

"I'd think that would get old after a while."

Very old. But she couldn't tell him that. Instead she forced a light, careless tone. "Hilly and I are happy." Then she changed the subject. "What about you? Where did you begin professionally?"

He sat up, leaning his forearms on his thighs. "I started here in Colorado, as a reporter and then editor of a small newspaper up in Grand Lake. That's a mountain town in case you're not familiar with it. Eventually I bought the owner out, turned it from a barely read little rag into a thriving newspaper and sold it for a profit. From there I basically did the same thing—picking up small, failing papers, reviving them and reselling them. Along the way I've kept a few and added a magazine here and there."

There was no arrogance or bragging in what he said even though there was room for it. "How many do you own?"

"Nine newspapers. *Probe* will be my fourth magazine, if I can find a good enough story to get it off the ground."

"Is that what you were doing in New York for so long?"

He shook his head. "I had a financial magazine based there that could have used your reorganizational talents," he finished in a lighter vein.

"You can't believe everything Hilly says about that. She's biased."

He sat up straight and turned toward her, bracing himself on one hand that rested behind her. The change in position brought him much closer. "Oh, I don't know. I think I'm more inclined to think you're too humble." With his other hand he reached to toy with a wisp of her hair that curled from her temple. "I think that maybe a surprise job failure has left you doubting yourself. Don't let it."

The compassion, understanding and support in his voice touched her.

Then he went on. "I'd hate to think that any day now you might disappear. I really want to get to know you."

That stabbed her and Mitch realized it was because for the first time in more than three years she wished that was possible. "There's not that much to know," she replied because she had to.

His hand left her hair to feather-stroke her temple. "Would you let me try to show you how good it can be to become involved again...in a permanent job and maybe even in a life other than just Hilly's?"

He was reaching something in her that Mitch hadn't been in touch with for a long, long time. A part of her that she had put to sleep in favor of leaving everything but Hilly behind. She turned her face to him, feeling a softness and a warmth she barely remembered. But still she answered, "No. I can't," in a voice weak with a lack of conviction.

"Sure you can," he coaxed.

Then he cupped the back of her head and brought her toward him. Meeting her halfway, his mouth covered hers. At first the kiss was as tentative as it had been the last time, but it didn't stay that way long. His lips parted slightly over hers. His tongue urged her mouth open and when she complied he traced just the tips of her teeth.

His arms came around her, pulling her close. Mitch gave in to him and to her own feelings, letting herself be held against that broad chest, even hooking her arms up under his and splaying her hands over his hard back. The person she had been a long time ago awakened and leaned into his kiss, savoring the taste of him, the scent of his after-shave mingling with her own perfume, the slightly moist, slipperiness of his mouth. It felt so wonderful to be held by him and to hold him in return.

Too wonderful.

She couldn't be the person she had been before. She couldn't succumb to these feelings. She couldn't let him into her heart knowing the time would come when she would have to wrench herself away.

She ended the kiss and pushed out of his arms, shaking her head as if she hadn't been fully aware of what she was doing, as if it had just dawned on her. "I don't want this," and then she repeated it because the first time it had sounded as if she was trying to convince herself rather than him.

He cleared his throat and in the dim light Mitch thought for the second time that night that he looked the way she felt, as if he was just coming up for air from feelings that had overtaken him as well, feelings that didn't sit any easier with him than they did with her.

She heard him draw a deep breath and hold it, as though to regain control. Then he exhaled and shook his head. "Powerful stuff at work here, isn't it?"

Too powerful, Mitch thought.

"I meant what I said, Mitch. I want to get to know you."

Her mind was shouting no, but she couldn't make the word come out, and ended just shaking her head in denial.

She didn't know if he hadn't seen it in the darkness or if he just chose to ignore it, for he stood up from the picnic table and said in an emotion-ragged voice, "Tomorrow at nine. Dress casually—we aren't formal even at the office." He kissed her fleetingly once more and disappeared into the shadows of the hedge before she heard the gate creak open and close.

Powerful and dangerous, she thought, reminding herself forcefully that there was more than just her heart at risk here.

As he closed the gate behind him and headed for his house Patrick could hear his phone ringing. He'd left his door unlocked and so rushed in and managed to answer it before it stopped.

"It's about time. I've been calling you all night," Les said to Patrick's hello.

"Gosh, Dad, I didn't know I was supposed to stay home," he responded with heavy sarcasm.

"Well, let's watch it from here on."

"What's up?"

"One of our guys got a hot tip he wants to follow and I thought you might want to know about it before I give the go-ahead. It's a long shot."

"Let's hear it."

"Seems there's a man in Alabama who reputedly lived a peaceful, socially conscious life for the past sixty-five years and has suddenly been convicted of five grisly murders. He swears he's innocent and the whole community is behind him. Some of the evidence against him was insubstantial and he has an alibi for four out of five of the crimes. But the last victim was the mayor's son. There was heavy pressure to find someone to pin it on and this old guy has taken the fall."

Patrick thought about it. "Not bad."

"What do you mean not bad? If it's the truth and we break it open, *Probe* couldn't have a better launch."

"*If* it's true. Send some of our people down there to look into it."

"That's what I wanted to hear."

"Les," Patrick called him back from hanging up. "Did your cousin the chemical engineer in Seattle ever get another job?"

"Nothing substantial enough to pay his house payment, no. Why?"

"I've been thinking about something else that might work for us."

"Something as juicy as my Alabama frame-up?"

"No, something with a broader spectrum. Even if yours pans out we might be able to consider this for the second issue. I've spent some time this weekend with Al's house sitters. I don't have any details, but the picture I'm getting is of a well-educated, capable, intelligent woman who lost a good job and ended up losing everything, as your cousin would have if it hadn't been for your help. There's been a lot of focus on the home-less who are runaways or derelicts or drunks or drug addicts or the mentally ill, but how many are victims of a declining economy? People who really worked for their futures, who got themselves educated and paid their dues and still ended up on the streets?''

''Al's house sitters are homeless?''

''Looks that way. Mitch has a heavy dose of pride, so she won't say much, but it's clear that she's a long way from what anyone would expect of a person who works odd jobs to support herself and her grandmother, all the while having to move from place to place to do it.''

''What would our focus be?''

''The idea is too new for details, but we could inves-tigate just how much of this is happening, what's being done to utilize people who have education and experi-ence, what kind of networking, if any, exists to get them help. Maybe we could get the ball rolling if there's nothing out there for them. Think about it.''

''The pride element is nothing to ignore. My cousin washes dishes in a greasy spoon but nobody who isn't close to him knows that. I doubt that he'd want it pub-lished in a national magazine.''

''Even if it got him a job in his field?''

''I'd have to discuss it with him. How about Al's house sitter? I'd think the same would go for her if she's too proud to even talk about it.''

''I told you, this is a fledgling idea. I'm not even ab-solutely sure this is her story. Why don't you put some-body on digging up any information. For now we'll concentrate on your Alabama lead.''

After Patrick hung up he poured himself a glass of iced tea and took it out back. He didn't turn on any lights and instead sat in the dark, facing the hedge that separated his house from Al's.

Was Mitch still on the other side, he wondered, or had she gone in?

Picturing her in the scenario he had just outlined for Les—the image he'd had as she talked tonight—gave him the same feelings that had caused him to start *Probe* in the first place. Working in the news business had brought him too often into contact with bad things happening to good people. He had found it unbearably frustrating to stand by helplessly watching the havoc that could be wreaked on an innocent person's life. For some reason that feeling was even stronger now that it was Mitch who made up the picture.

He didn't believe her claim to be a free spirit. That was her pride talking, he thought. It seemed to him that she was covering up deep feelings of failure caused by losing a good job she had relied on. Turning down his offer of helping her to find permanent work in favor of living nomadically seemed protective. If she never settled in one place or had to commit herself to making a go at one job again, she didn't run the risk of repeating that failure.

How was that for armchair analysis?

But was it true? And if it was, would it color her personal relationships, too?

It already had, he realized. She was anything but anxious for any kind of involvement with him.

Well, at least she wasn't a gold digger.

For the first time since a year ago instant anger wasn't his reaction to a reference to Amy and the con she had played on him. In fact he felt somewhat removed, and that took him by surprise.

Testing himself, he thought about the tip-off that had alerted him to how she had been married twice before and had divorced her husbands as soon as she could get them to a community property state and claim half of their assets.

Still Patrick felt nothing.

She had fooled him, he goaded.

Before, there had been little comfort in being in good company. But now he found it reassuring that both of his predecessors had been intelligent, successful men whose reputations, accomplishments and contributions to society he respected. Now he thought that love could blind the best of them.

There was a strong sense of satisfaction in knowing he was past not only his love for Amy, but his anger and hurt as well. His only lingering sense of disquiet was in wondering how a person knew when they were being blinded.

Comparison, maybe?

Was Mitch anything like Amy?

Not in any outward way.

But weren't Mitch and Hilly doing about the same thing Amy had? After all, they were living in Al's house rent free. What if their answer to losing everything, to being homeless, was to find someone to provide for them, the way Amy had latched onto him? Granted, it seemed more acceptable for Mitch and Hilly, at least in the scenario he had devised for them. But what if they were every bit as conniving as Amy had been? What if the reason Mitch was so standoffish was because she didn't want him interfering with their plans?

Patrick shook his head and sighed, disgusted with himself. Was he going to spend the rest of his life looking for hidden agendas in everyone he came across just because he'd found it in one woman? That was a great mind-set for someone starting a magazine designed to be a crusader, wasn't it?

But chastising himself didn't make the doubts dissolve.

So many things about Mitch and Hilly seemed unexplained. And Mitch was so reticent about revealing anything. Was it just admirable pride? Or was she hiding something not so admirable?

He wanted to believe it was admirable pride because he was so damned attracted to her. Because he liked her and Hilly so much. But maybe wanting to believe was the first step in being blinded.

*So what are you going to do about it, Drake?*

Tread carefully was the only answer he could come up with. Keep his eyes and ears open. Because he couldn't deny what he had learned from the experience with Amy any more than he could deny this pull he felt toward Mitch.

He heard Hilly calling for her.

"Coming," she answered, and he listened to the sounds of her going inside.

It couldn't be true that Mitch and Hilly were like Amy, he thought. And yet he knew that until all of his questions were answered he also couldn't be absolutely sure that they weren't.

## Chapter Four

It was a rare occasion when Mitch woke up earlier than Hilly. But it happened that morning. The clock on her night table read four-fifty-four a.m., and she was wide awake.

After three years of changing jobs regularly, starting a new one didn't give her enough jitters to wake her up nearly four hours before she needed to be there. No, the adrenaline that made Mitch's heart race was not coming from that. For a moment she tried to pin it on Hilly's Friday night sighting of a shadow in the bushes. But it was hard to lie to herself.

The real reason was pure anticipation over the prospect of spending the day with Patrick. And she was disgusted with herself for it.

Maybe it was Denver's high altitude that made heads and hearts light and therefore more vulnerable, she thought, preferring that explanation for why she and

Hilly should be struck with the same weakness. Nothing like this had happened to them during the whole time they had been on the move. Sea level was where they had better stay from here on.

By a quarter after five Mitch gave up trying to go back to sleep, and got up. Assuring herself that it was just to fill time, she took another scented bubble bath and washed her hair again. She pressed white slacks and a teal green camp shirt that didn't really need it, then spent forty-five minutes fixing her hair while telling herself that there had been other days like this. Getting the tortoise-shell combs to hold back the sides just right sometimes required several attempts. And hadn't she taken almost as much pains with her makeup last night when she hadn't known Patrick would be there? It wasn't for him. It really wasn't.

Not much it wasn't.

Maybe she should play sick and stay home, she thought. Spending time with him was courting danger, and her life teetered on the edge enough as it was. The last thing she needed was to take a step closer to destruction.

Nip it in the bud, she told herself firmly. Get forceful with Hilly and insist that she stop pushing the two of you together. Don't do this to yourself. Don't let it go any further. Don't get in any deeper. Run.

Oh, but she was tired of running.

When had that happened? She hadn't noticed the feeling before, this longing for a stable life again, for staying in one place, for building a future. Why now? Was it just Patrick? Or was there more to it?

Mitch took a deep breath and held it for a moment.

The reasons didn't matter. Nothing mattered but that she and Hilly couldn't stop running no matter how much either of them might want to. Thinking about it and wanting it would only make the running worse.

She wished she could get Hilly out of bed, load the clock into the hearse and get out of here today, this morning, right now.

Mitch picked up the telephone and put her index finger on the button that would automatically dial Patrick's number.

Call and tell him you aren't coming, she ordered herself. And then spend this whole day convincing Hilly it's time to leave. Now. Before Alfred gets home and she gets in any deeper either.

*Do it.*

*Don't be stupid. Do it.*

Her eyes suddenly burned like fire and she closed them. Her heart was beating fast and hard.

There wasn't a single doubt in her mind that she should get Hilly and herself as far away from Colorado—and Alfred and Patrick—as she could. That premonition Friday night hadn't been about the past catching up with them again. It had been about meeting Patrick. She knew it. And feelings that strong shouldn't be ignored.

"Do it," she whispered to herself.

But she couldn't.

Slowly she hung up.

She was convinced she'd lost her mind. She had to be insane to stay here and chance so much.

Mitch sat down on the bed feeling as if she were deflating. No matter how many times she told herself she shouldn't, she knew she was going to stay here for now. She also knew she was going to go next door and spend today with Patrick, that she couldn't resist the attraction she felt for him, that she had to have just a little time with him to get to know him.

And if she suffered for it later? She would just have to deal with that when it happened. All she could hope for was that when later came it didn't devastate more than just her heart.

It was five minutes before nine when Mitch went through the gate in the hedge to Patrick's house. He must have been watching for her because by the time she walked up to the back door he had opened it for her. He was on the phone and motioned for her to come in.

The smell of fresh coffee was redolent in the air, and though she and Hilly never drank it, Mitch loved the aroma. Probably because it was a memory from a time before her parents were killed. To her it seemed homey and somehow masculine, as if only houses with men smelled of brewed coffee in the morning.

Patrick rolled his eyes and shrugged to let her know he was sorry he couldn't get off the phone. Mitch shook her head and waved away his apology, then found her gaze stuck on him. He was wearing khaki slacks, a cream-colored, button-down shirt and well-polished loafers with tassels. Although still casual he looked more businesslike than she had yet seen him, and she was glad she hadn't worn anything more informal than the white slacks and camp shirt.

Not wanting to eavesdrop on his conversation, Mitch wandered into the hallway to look at the pictures that were hanging. The photographs were of other people. A marked resemblance made it easy enough to assume that most of them were his family. As near as Mitch could tell, he had gray-haired parents, a brother and a sister, both married, with three children for the brother and two for the sister.

On the wall were also half a dozen drawings, all matted and richly framed. They seemed incongruous since they were a child's crayon renditions of houses, trees and people.

"Admiring my art collection?" Patrick asked as he came to stand beside her.

"Did you do these?"

He grinned at her. "Displaying my own crayon drawings would be egotistical. My sister's youngest daughter is the artist, and she's very serious about her work. You have to earn the honor of being given one drawing, and she expects it to be treated with the significance she's convinced it deserves."

"You must really rate highly to have so many," Mitch observed with a smile, appreciating the fact that he treated the child's feelings so conscientiously.

The way his grin widened told her how fond he was of his niece. "She's a character—not too unlike your grandmother. And I've always been a sucker for people who are just slightly off-center. Elizabeth is nine now and has moved on to abstract work. She glues curlicue pencil shavings or crayon scrapings to paper these days. I have to keep those flat."

"Of course," she answered with mock gravity. Then she smiled. "Do you come from a close family?"

"I'd call it close, yes. Even though they're all still in Grand Lake and I travel more than I'd like, I manage to get up there about once a month. And we talk on the phone a lot more often than that."

Mitch indicated a picture of the two people she assumed to be his brother and sister, with Patrick standing between them, an arm around each. The background was nondescript trees. "Where are you in that birth order?"

"Oldest. Then comes my sister Melanie—she just turned thirty-five—and Brian, the baby at thirty-four." He paused a moment. "How about you? Any hot and heavy sibling rivalry in your life?"

She and George were a long way from being siblings but what was between them could probably be considered a rivalry. Only to call it hot and heavy was putting it mildly. Rather than offering that bit of information, Mitch shook her head and told him the simple truth. "I was an only child."

"There were times when I wished I was," he joked. "How about cousins?"

"Only distant ones—cousins of my parents and their kids. I'm never sure how they rank. But I haven't seen any of them for years and years. We were never close."

"So does that mean there's just you and Hilly?"

"Yes," she lied, and before he could get into another one of his inquisitions, she stepped away from the wall and faced him. "Shouldn't we get to work?"

"How about a cup of coffee first?"

"Never touch the stuff. Hilly says it eats your stomach lining."

"Tea then?"

"I've had mine already this morning." Actually she'd had nearly a whole pot of Hilly's chamomile. It was supposed to calm the nerves. Unfortunately it hadn't done anything with her unnerving, intensified awareness of this man.

"Let me get a fresh cup and I'll show you the house before we get started. It didn't occur to me until after you had left Saturday night that I didn't do it then. My mother would be disappointed to know that I had forgotten one of her first rules—always show a guest around so they can get to the bathroom when they need to. She instigated it when one of my friends who was spending the night had wandered into my parents' bedroom at an indelicate moment in search of the facilities."

Mitch laughed and grimaced at once. "I'll bet it was a long time before you got to have anyone spend the night again."

"No, they were pretty good about it. I just had to make sure from then on that I gave the house tour first thing." He went into the kitchen for his coffee and came right back. As he passed close behind her in the hallway, he squeezed her upper arm. "Come on, I'll do my duty now before I forget again and leave you walking in on something indelicate."

"Thank you. I'd appreciate being spared that," she deadpanned. The spot on her arm still tingled long after he had let go of her.

He stepped into the room at the other end of the hall. "This is the family room. It lacks a family, but it's still a room."

And a beautiful one at that. The expansive space was carpeted in a plush brown shag. Around an oval coffee table was a comfortable-looking eight-section U-shaped sofa with plump pillows lining the back and arms. Two overstuffed chairs angled toward a stone fireplace with a carved mantel. The walls were paneled and two of the three were lined with bookshelves that housed an impressive collection of hardback books separated by an assortment of sculptures, ceramic bowls, and high up on one shelf, a golf trophy.

To Mitch it was the perfect room, artfully decorated and yet warm and inviting. It was actually cozy, in a way she didn't expect a man's house to be. She preferred it to Alfred's very formal furnishings.

"This is nice," she complimented, meaning it. "I can just see you sitting with your feet on the coffee table watching that big-screen TV in the corner while your daughter daydreams in front of a roaring fire and your two sons wrestle with their draft horse of a dog behind the couch."

She was teasing and yet as she said it it became a very vivid picture in her mind, with herself sitting close beside him, reading one of those books from his shelves. It was irrational, but a wave of the most potent sadness washed through her.

"Now that is a sexist description," he teased her back, his deep, amused voice helping to draw her out of the darker feelings.

"You want your daughter wrestling with the draft horse of a dog and your sons daydreaming?" she played along.

"Or my daughter wrestling with my sons and the draft horse of a dog daydreaming?"

"Perfect." Mitch laughed and realized that for the first time since they'd met she was beginning to honestly relax with him.

They moved on to the formal living and dining rooms, still more casually decorated than Alfred's house.

"Now we get into the personal stuff," he warned her in a stage whisper as he took her elbow. "This is the laundry room, just in case you have a laundry emergency."

"I don't have many of those."

"This bathroom is for company," he explained as he went. Glancing back over his shoulder as if there were someone there he said, "See, Mom, I didn't forget." Then he urged Mitch to poke her head in each of the four bedrooms, all with their own baths, before leading the way into the master room, in the center of which was the biggest bed she had ever seen.

"Is this for orgies or what?" she asked before she realized what she was saying.

"I beg your pardon." He pretended to be shocked, but his grin was too wide to make it convincing.

"I've never seen a bed that big," she tried to amend the slip of her tongue with an explanation.

"It has to be big enough for three kids and a draft horse of a dog to climb into on snowy mornings."

Another instant image that was painfully wonderful to Mitch. "Of course," she agreed quickly to keep up the repartee and hide her feelings of regret that it was all something she would never have.

"And there hasn't been a single orgy on it," he said, seeming to delight in not letting her off the hook. "Of course if you were suggesting..."

Mitch spun toward a door beside the bed. "I'll bet this is another bathroom," she said in a hurry.

"Of course. But that one probably isn't clean."

Too late, Mitch had already stepped into the doorway. He was right; it wasn't clean. There was a used bath towel slung over a beveled glass shower door that was half-open. Behind it was a huge oval bathtub that took three steps to get into. A smaller towel was in a heap on the tiled floor, and yet another was draped across the back of a mirror marked with dried water rivulets. In the center was a smudge where he must have wiped away steam to see into it after his shower. Through a high and wide rectangular window she could see the blue umbrella that shaded the glass table on the back patio. A stick of deodorant was on the sill. Littering the counter was shaving cream and razor, and an open bottle of after-shave that scented the triple-size bathroom with the smell Mitch had come to think of as Patrick's.

Another pang of sadness hit her. Of all places, she thought, in a messy bathroom. But there it was, almost stronger than it had been the other two times. She spun around and forced brightness. "So where do we work?"

"Does that mean the orgy is out?"

"Definitely."

"Damn." He grinned at her. "Then my office is through those double doors on the other side of the bed. I had it put as far away from where those two sons, the daughter and the draft horse of a dog would be making noise."

He said it as easily as if her description actually was what he had had in mind in the building of this house. Then she realized that raising a family here must have been a part of the plan. The fact that he was family oriented rather than goal and money oriented was just another thing about him that appealed to her. But, "Lead the way," was all she said, at the same time wishing that she could find more things that made him less attractive and fewer things that increased his appeal.

He had been right about needing some help sorting and filing papers. The walls of his office were lined with filing cabinets and shelves, all of which were cluttered with stacks of files spilling paper. In the center of the disarray was a walnut desk, the top obscured by more of the same.

"See why I needed a girl Friday today?"

"It goes without saying." Mitch went in ahead of him, stopping at the front of the desk to survey the job she had taken on. "What was that you said about organization being your long suit?"

"*Corporate* reorganization, not *filing* reorganization."

"Ah, my mistake."

He came up behind her and took her shoulders in his hands. He bent to her ear, and she could feel the warm breath there. "Have I daunted you?"

The mess she could handle. His touching her was something else. Even if it was only casual and friendly to him, to her it was igniting little fires in every spot of contact. It was hard to concentrate when she was singeing from the inside out.

Mitch made a show of snapping to attention and saluting to get herself out of his grasp. "No, sir. Ready for cleanup duty, sir."

He glanced around the room, making a face at the mess. "I don't know. Now that you've brought it up, I think I'd really rather have an orgy."

"Forget the orgy," she told him with mock sternness. "And just tell me where to start and what to do with all of this."

"Spoilsport." He sighed wistfully, winked at her and then gave her instructions.


By noon Mitch and Patrick had cleared up the majority of the mess in his office and headed to the Tech Center in his sleek white sports car. The phone it was equipped with rang within two blocks of home and, with apologies to Mitch, he spent the drive there settling some dispute within his New York publication, hanging up only as he parked in a space with his name on it.

The offices for *Probe* took up the entire third floor of one of the black-glass buildings that made up Denver's Tech Center complex. As they passed several computer-supplied cubicles to get to Patrick's office he was greeted with a warmth and friendliness that gave Mitch the impression that his employees liked both their jobs and their boss.

"Hello, Nora, you gorgeous thing," Patrick said as he rounded a desk and came up behind a tall, thin, blond woman filing papers in a row of black cabinets.

The woman spun around. Her attractive, perfectly made-up oval face seemed to beam with pleasure as she looked at Patrick, only to dim considerably when he introduced Mitch and explained why she was with him.

"I told you I didn't mind working overtime to help you out with that," the secretary said a little tightly.

"I couldn't have you doing that," Patrick vetoed with aplomb. "You serve above and beyond the call of duty as it is. I felt like I was taking advantage of you by having you arrange for someone to open up my house and stock it with groceries. When I found out you did it yourself I felt like a heel. But thanks. You did a great job, as always."

Mitch wondered if Patrick saw the adoration in the other woman's eyes. But whether he did or not, she did. And it ruffled something inside her, as if she were a cat whose fur had been rubbed the wrong way.

"What'll you have, Mitch? Ham or turkey?"

It took her a moment to catch up to the conversation and register that Patrick had asked his secretary to order them sandwiches for lunch. "Turkey," she chose quickly, hoping she hadn't let too much time lapse. Then Patrick opened a nearby door and waited for her to go in ahead of him.

This office was not nearly as disorganized as his home one had been. The top of his L-shaped walnut desk was visible in spots, only a few disks littered the computer and printer area, and a single stack of papers waited on the filing cabinet.

"Don't be fooled because it looks better," he said as if he had been privy to her thoughts. "Most of what I need you to do is make hard copy off the disks and then file it. I hope Hilly wasn't just bragging when she said you were a whiz with a computer."

"I don't think you have to be a whiz to print out some files," she said distractedly. She was listening to him with half of her brain at the same time the other part was assimilating new facts—like an extremely attractive secretary who was obviously more fond of Patrick than mere employer-employee relations required; like the fact that the woman had enough familiarity with him to go into his house to clean it while he was away; like the fact that Patrick had greeted her as *Nora, you gorgeous thing*...

Just then a tall, tank of a man stormed through the door without knocking. "It's about time you got your butt in here you old son of a—" He stopped short when he caught sight of Mitch. "Whoops. Sorry, didn't know you had company," he finished with an ear-to-ear grin that made a lie out of the apology.

"This, Mitch, is Les Burns—"

Before Patrick could say any more Les Burns finished, "I'm the man behind the man. His right hand. He couldn't do squat without me." His glance ran from the top of Mitch's head to her toes and back again. "And by the color of your hair and eyes I'd say you're Al's house sitter."

*Patrick had told him the color of her hair and eyes?*
It went a long way toward soothing her ruffled feath-
ers.

Patrick finished his interrupted introduction. "This
is Mitch Cuddy. I've hired her to organize me."

Les Burns extended a hammy hand her way. As Mitch
took it and said hello she thought that the ruddy com-
plexioned, balding, black-haired man looked more as
though he belonged on a football field than in an office.

"Les and I and Al and one of Al's cronies make up a
foursome in golf. That's how Les knows Al," Patrick
explained. Then he said pointedly to his friend, who was
still staring at Mitch, "Didn't you say you were on your
way out?"

"No, I don't think I did," Les replied with a laugh.
But he took two steps backward toward the door anyway, his gaze staying on Mitch. Then he looked at Patrick. "I sent some of our people to Alabama but I
haven't put anyone on that other idea of yours yet. I'll
get to it this afternoon."

"Great. Just keep me informed."

Les slid a glance Mitch's way again and then back to
Patrick. "Nice," he murmured approvingly, leaving
only to be replaced by Nora bearing their lunch order.

After the warm reception by Les, Mitch had the sensation of a chill coming into the room. As Nora set their
sandwiches on the coffee table in the center of a long
leather couch and two matching chairs, she exchanged
a few words with Patrick. But all the while she ignored
Mitch as thoroughly as if she were invisible. Only when
it was obvious there was no more reason for her to stay
did she go out to her own desk, leaving the office door
wide open.

Patrick closed it. "I would have liked to take you out to a long, lingering lunch, but we'd never get this finished if I did. I owe you, though."

"I didn't expect anything like that. In fact, I don't mind eating at the desk while we work." Actually she preferred it rather than having to make conversation when the only thing she could think about was Patrick's secretary and what their relationship might entail.

"You're sure?

"Positive."

He set her up at the computer but before he could do anything more Nora came in to tell him he was needed in the research department. Taking his sandwich with him, Patrick left and Mitch went to work on her own. She tried not to think about the smug expression on the secretary's face just before she made a show of shutting the door this time, effectively closing Mitch in.

The remainder of the afternoon went much the same. Each time Patrick came into the office he was called out again within minutes. By the fourth time he shrugged and said to Mitch, "Now you can see why I work out of my home more often than here. I never get anything done when I come in."

No thanks to your secretary, Mitch thought, as she went on working without him.

With the lion's share of the filing finished by five Patrick insisted they stop for the day. On their way out Nora made it very clear that she could handle what was left and Mitch thought it was just as well. The other woman had effectively negated Mitch's first impression of this office as being a nice place to work.

"What's on your agenda for tonight?" Patrick asked on the way home.

"Hilly and I are going to do some cleaning and get things spruced up for Alfred's homecoming." It was a lie. That was what Hilly had planned to do herself during the day, but Mitch thought that spending any more time with Patrick was pushing her luck. His effect on her was too powerful.

Conversely she was disappointed when he accepted her excuse. As she told him goodbye and closed the car door she couldn't help wondering if he would call Nora and ask her to keep him company instead, and for a moment considered rescinding her refusal.

Jealousy, that's what this is, she realized as she unlocked the front door of Alfred's house. Plain, old, run-of-the-mill jealousy.

And even telling herself that it was ridiculous and out of place didn't make it go away.

Patrick watched Mitch go into Alfred's house before he rounded the curve and pulled into his own driveway. He hadn't put up an argument over not seeing her that night because he already had a counterattack for her denial. He would take a shower, change his clothes and then go next door to pay her for her day's work. Hilly would do the rest, or at least aid and abet him in spending the evening with Mitch. He felt pleased with himself.

As he waited for the automatic opener to raise the garage door he saw Alfred's silver car coming up the street. It was a welcome sight. Now he could find out just how much his friend knew about Mitch and Hilly. Maybe some of his suspicions would be put to rest.

Patrick pulled into the garage, turned off the car and got out. But rather than going into the house he headed next door and found Alfred opening the trunk of his own car.

"Patrick! Good to see you back finally," the wiry little man called as Patrick crossed the yards.

"How'd you do in the tournament?" Patrick asked with a nod to the golf clubs in the trunk.

"Third," Alfred groaned. He was nearly a foot shorter than Patrick, had only half a head of white hair, a face as creased with wrinkles as a peach pit, and large ears that stuck out even farther with the weight of his snazzy sunglasses. "My mind wasn't on my game."

"I noticed you were pretty busy beefing up your social life while I was in New York," Patrick teased him, glancing toward the house.

"Everything all right since Friday night?"

"Fine. I think the whole thing started with a dream Hilly had."

"Can't understand it. It's not like Hilly to be excitable."

"Well, nothing came of it, so I don't suppose it matters." Patrick lifted the golf clubs out of the trunk for the older man. "I understand you met at a funeral."

That made Alfred laugh. "Can you beat it? Best damn thing that ever happened to me at one of those."

"And you've been together ever since, have you?"

"Not as together as I'd like us to be."

"Oh?"

"If I had my way Hilly and I'd be cruising the Caribbean on our honeymoon right now."

"Why you old dog," Patrick laughed, belying the disquiet that information made him feel. "So why aren't you?"

Alfred made a face that pulled the corners of his mouth down nearly to his chin. "Hilly's worried what would happen to Mitch if she married me. They're quite a twosome, you know.''

''So I've gathered. But what is Hilly afraid would happen to Mitch if the two of you were married?''

''Oh, I don't know. I keep telling her it's just plain silly. I guess Hilly feels like she'd be abandoning Mitch. Of course I told her that Mitchy could live with us, or I'd even pay for an apartment for her if she didn't want to stay with two old coots. It doesn't matter to me that they aren't related by blood. But Hilly's afraid Mitch's pride wouldn't let her agree to either of those ideas, that she might go off traveling by herself the way they've been doing together. I hope it never comes down to Hilly choosing between the two of us because I'm liable to be history.''

At first Patrick didn't think he had heard him right. ''Hilly isn't Mitch's grandmother?''

''Oh, no. But that's an honest assumption,'' the older man assured him, taking a puff on his pipe. ''I thought the same thing when I first met them. But they're not related at all.''

Patrick lifted Alfred's suitcase out onto the driveway, digesting this information. ''I understood that Hilly raised Mitch after her parents were killed.''

''She did.''

At least that much was true. ''Well, why would she do that if they aren't related?''

''The way I understand it, Hilly was good friends with Mitch's parents before their death. If you've been around my girl you know how spunky she is, so it didn't surprise me at all to hear she had friends young enough to be her own kids. Anyway, when Mitch's folks died there were some pretty seedy cousins wanting to take her in and Hilly said she just couldn't stand by and watch it. So she took her and raised her as if she was her granddaughter. They're just that close, too. Maybe closer." Al slammed the trunk of his car shut. "But don't give up on me yet. I'm putting everything I have into convincing Hilly to marry me."

Putting everything the older man had on the line was just what Patrick was afraid of. Maybe just what Mitch and Hilly were counting on, he thought.

Just then the front door of his house flew open and Hilly came out. "Alfred!" she called, throwing her arms straight up in the air before she rushed toward them and clasped the older man in an energetic bear hug. "You're home early."

"Couldn't see any reason to stay over another night when I had you to come home to."

Patrick readjusted the golf clubs rather than watch the older couple kiss.

"Let's celebrate." Hilly's exuberant suggestion told him it was safe to look again. "What do you say the four of us go out dancing tonight? You do dance, don't you, Patrick? Mitch loves it."

Patrick's thoughts had been headed in a different direction and this took him by surprise. He glanced at Alfred to see if it was agreeable to him and found the older man smiling broadly.

"Sounds great to me. Let's go for dinner first and make a night of it," Alfred said.

"Sure," Patrick answered a little foggily.

"Wonderful." Hilly clapped her hands.

Then Patrick put in, "But maybe we'd better ask Mitch before we make it definite."

Hilly's laugh cut Patrick off. "And give her the chance to come up with an excuse? That's not the way to handle her. I'll just tell her we're all going dancing and she has to come."

That seemed to settle it. They agreed on Patrick coming over in an hour and Hilly and Alfred took the suitcase and golf clubs rather than let him help with them.

"Come all dressed up," Hilly called to him as he headed home. "She won't be able to resist you."

Patrick waved in answer. But as he let himself into his own house what he was going to wear was not on his mind. Instead he was wondering what had actually been happening Friday night to prompt Mitch and Hilly to lie about their relationship.

It wasn't reassuring to realize that rather than having some of his suspicions put to rest, he now had even more.

## Chapter Five

Patrick was just coming out of the shower a half an hour later when the phone rang. The fact that it took four rings before it occurred to him to answer it was an indication of how preoccupied he was by the news that Hilly was not really Mitch's grandmother. But by the fifth ring he picked it up.

"How come you left the office so early?" Les's voice answered his hello. "I came looking for you at five after five and you were gone with the wind."

"I had to get out of there before I fired Nora for driving me nuts. She was like a duckling after its mother. Where I went, she went. And every time I managed to get back to my office without her she trumped up some reason why I had to come out again."

Les laughed. "That's what you get for bringing competition onto her battlefield. Or did you think all that loyalty and devotion came from wanting to be a good employee?''

"Since you seem to know so much about Nora, maybe you ought to find a way of gently getting it across to her that I'm not interested.''

"Because you *are* interested in Mitch, is that it?'' Les goaded.

Patrick scowled at his friend's words. Before he could either agree or refute the statement, Les went on.

"I can't blame you. I like your lady. She's a class act.''

"Mmm.'' His distraction was echoed in the murmur.

"Why do I sound more convinced than you do?''

"Did you just call to talk to me about women? Because if you did I have a date with one in half an hour and I won't make it if this takes too long.''

"Touchy, touchy. No, I called to let you know that my preliminaries show you might be right about the epidemic of middle-class unemployment. There are some indications that a whole new set of people are joining the ranks of the homeless.''

"And the con artists?''

"Sorry, I didn't catch that.''

"Nothing.''

"Okay. Well, I talked to my cousin and he shocked the hell out of me by being willing to let us feature him in the story, if we do it. Thought you'd want to know.''

*What I'd really like to know is what the hell is going on with Mitch and Hilly,* his mind responded. Maybe if he kept asking questions he could find out something that could shape it all up differently. Or maybe just time would help. Maybe she was a person who wasn't easily intimate with strangers. Maybe as they got to know each other better, as she came to be more comfortable with him, she would start to open up.

"I said, I thought you'd want to know," Les's voice called him back from his thoughts.

It took Patrick a minute to remember what they were talking about. "Go ahead with some general statistical research about how widespread it is, where it's the worst, if there's anything being done to help this group get back into the mainstream. But I don't want any investigation into Mitch's background done yet."

"Huh? Who said anything about investigating Mitch's background?"

Patrick closed his eyes in a grimace. No one had said anything about it. It was just a thought niggling at the back of his mind that had somehow found a way out his mouth.

Les went on. "We wouldn't do that for the story if she doesn't want to be a part of it, would we?"

*Think fast.* "I just meant that we know the genuine circumstances of your cousin's situation. But even though Mitch is...special to me, we'd still have to verify her story the same way we do with everything before we take sides and print anything."

"So you know for sure now that she's in the same boat as my cousin? She's confided in you?"

"No." Patrick pinched the bridge of his nose. He was fumbling and he knew it. Apparently so did Les.

"Are you worrying that Mitch is a rerun of Amy? Is that why having her investigated is on your mind?"

"You know how it is," Patrick shrugged off his friend's concern. "When one relationship goes bad all your antennae are programmed to watch out for that same thing in the next one. Pride makes her pretty closemouthed. That's all it is. After Amy I'm just too sensitive to anything that even seems like secrecy." Then before Les could pursue it Patrick went back to talking about work. "Anyway, just get some initial data together. I don't think this is juicy enough for the launch issue under any circumstances. Your murder is better. How's that coming?"

"Nothing yet."

"Well, let's hope it pans out."

Patrick hung up and went back into the bathroom to shave, but the slip of his tongue about having Mitch investigated stayed with him. The idea had come to him in conjunction with the article but he knew himself well enough to know that this had nothing to do with business.

He had hated having Amy investigated. It had felt so sleazy. So low. So paranoid. But it had given him answers she wouldn't. And now here he was with Mitch.

The practice of fact-checking every story made having her investigated palatable. But he knew the real reason for doing it was that it might uncover any more lies she had told him. It might offer some explanation for why she would lie in the first place.

"Damn," he said to the mirror as he combed his hair.

Just then through his open bathroom window he heard Mitch's distinctive laugh from Alfred's patio. Instantly he had a picture of her in his mind and a rush of feelings ran through him. She was already under his skin.

Did he want to know about her past? About her background?

He did if it was all innocent and aboveboard.

He didn't if it was going to put Mitch in Amy's league.

But if she was innocent and aboveboard he didn't need to know. And if she was in Amy's league he—and Al—did need to know, whether they liked it or not.

He heard Mitch laugh again and again his body reacted on cue. He wanted her, but he had to admit to himself that he didn't trust her.

Patrick patted after-shave on his face. The cold sting on his freshly shaved skin jolted him and a more rational side of this internal argument emerged.

Wasn't it too soon to do something as drastic as bringing an investigator in?

Of course it was. He might be falling fast, his attraction to her running at full speed, but the reality was that this relationship was still very new.

A little time. A little gentle persuasion. Gaining her trust. That was what was needed now. And what he was more than willing to put his energies into. The rest, including the story for *Probe*, could wait.

He turned around and leaned against the vanity, staring out the window. "Talk to me, Mitch," he entreated. "Tell me what the hell is going on to make you lie. Don't let me down."

Standing by the kitchen counter, Mitch was cleaning a smudge off her black satin evening bag. She couldn't remember when she had last felt this good and nothing she told herself in order to keep it under control helped. The fact was that for the first time in more than three years she was wearing the black crepe evening pants and sequined, backless top that she had bought in New York just a month before she and Hilly had begun their present life-style. And she was wearing it to go dancing with Patrick. For the moment, life didn't get any better than that.

Yes, his effect on her every sense was tantamount to a wrecking ball hitting the side of a decaying building. Her defenses were collapsing. Yes, every minute she was with him she liked him more—when she knew she shouldn't. And yes, if she was smart she would, at the very least, keep the time she spent with him to a minimum so she didn't get in any deeper than she already was.

But tonight she just didn't care. Tonight she was going to ignore all her cautions, live for the moment and let herself enjoy an evening—the likes of which she hadn't had in a long, long time and might never have again, with a man who made her feel things she had never felt before. Tonight was an island unto itself.

With that philosophy firmly in mind, she started transferring a few necessities from her daytime purse into the evening bag when she heard the creak of the gate in the hedge. That was all it took to make her heart beat hard and a flash of pleasure to skitter up the back of her arms.

She could tell he hadn't seen her as she unabashedly watched him cross the yard. He wore a dove-gray suit with a pale silver shirt and a mauve tie. She recognized the suit as Italian-made and by the way it fit his broad shoulders, narrow waist and long legs it was obvious it had been tailored for him. His hair glistened in the late sunshine and as he came up to the house on confident steps, with his back straight, he had the air of power about him.

*No wonder his secretary wants him.*

He raised a fist to knock on the sliding door but stopped when he caught sight of her. His face broke into a smile that weakened her knees and made her forget what she was doing. So much so, in fact, that she missed the countertop when she tried to set her daytime purse down and dropped it on the floor, spilling the contents.

She stepped over it and let him in.

"Wow," was the first thing he said, his tone full of admiration and his gaze sliding from the top of her wildly curly hair to her black shoes and back again. "You are . . . beautiful."

It sounded so much more genuine than his greeting to his secretary that Mitch forgave him for the earlier comment to the other woman. "Thank you, sir. You're not too hard on the eyes yourself."

He inclined his head in acknowledgement of the compliment. "Where are our lovebirds?"

"They're still dressing. Sit down while I clean up the mess I just made ogling you."

"Were you ogling me?" he answered, teasing with a crooked grin.

"Just a little," she said, flirting. She bent over to scoop her things into her purse, then stood. "I'll go up and tell them you're here."

"Don't be long," he answered with a seductive timbre in his voice.

Mitch was back in the kitchen ten minutes later. It surprised her to find Patrick standing and half facing the sliding glass door, with a frown as dark as any she had ever seen creasing his brow. "What's out there?"

His head jerked her way quickly, as if she had startled him. "Nothing, why?"

"You were smiling when I left and now I find you with such a serious expression on your face I thought you must have seen something to cause it."

He slipped his hand into his jacket pocket and smiled a bit wanly at her. "I was just thinking about an article

Les and I are considering for the second issue of
*Probe*." He seemed to draw himself out of those
thoughts, and went back to smiling, though the smile
looked halfhearted. "Are Hilly and Al about ready?"

It was Hilly who answered him from behind Mitch.
"We're here to dazzle you."

Compliments made the rounds for a few moments,
and then they decided that Patrick should drive Alfred's luxury car. The younger couple took the front
seat while the older one sat very close together in back,
holding hands and snuggling like two teenagers. With
Patrick still unusually quiet and the activities going on
behind her, Mitch was glad the restaurant was nearby.

Decorated in art deco, The Ritz served elaborate
meals in one wing of the U-shaped establishment and
had a live band for dancing in the other. Throughout
the lobster dinner the four of them enjoyed, Hilly mo-
nopolized the conversation, questioning Alfred and
Patrick about their relationship and golf, which she informed them she was very good at. Afraid that any
subject that involved her or Hilly might raise too many
questions about their past, Mitch steered the golf conversation back to Alfred's tournament.

Throughout the meal Patrick remained quiet. He
satisfied Hilly's curiosity whenever it was directed his
way, but seemed content not to offer too much more.
Mitch could feel him watching her, and had the sensation that he was trying to find an answer to something
by studying her. Twice when she caught him at it she
inclined her head and raised an eyebrow in silent question but both times he merely smiled at her and looked
away. By the time they left the restaurant and went into
the other wing Mitch couldn't help wondering what was
going on behind those penetrating, pale blue eyes.

One of the small booths that lined the ballroom walls had been reserved for them. While Hilly and Alfred headed out onto the expansive parquet dance floor, Mitch and Patrick sat and ordered the champagne Alfred had insisted they have.

Once the tuxedoed waiter had left them alone Patrick stretched his arm behind Mitch and leaned toward her, smiling. "Haven't we met somewhere before?"

It was the first time since Mitch had come back into Alfred's kitchen that Patrick sounded more like himself. She gratefully played along. "Sorry, you're not familiar. Was it years and years ago?"

"Yes, I believe we caught sight of each other somewhere between my meeting Al over a broken water pipe and the golf tournament Hilly won in 1953."

"Oh, I remember. How have you been?"

"I'm much better now that I have my date back, thanks."

The champagne arrived and Patrick told the waiter not to open it until the older couple had rejoined them.

"So what is this article you and Les are considering that made you look so serious before we left tonight?" Mitch asked, curious as to what had him so preoccupied.

He seemed to think about it a moment. When he answered it sounded as if he was feeling his way. "It would be a piece on how the economy has sucked some of the middle class into the ranks of the unemployed and homeless."

"That does sound grim."

He explained the situation with Les's cousin. "And then of course there's you and Hilly."

"Oh, no," she said too quickly. Then she concentrated on speaking more normally. "Hilly and I wouldn't want to be a part of anything like that."

"You say it as if I'm asking you to commit a crime with me."

This time she put finality in her voice. "We just couldn't do it. Hilly and I don't qualify for that, anyway. We do what we do by choice, not because there's nothing else we can do."

"But I thought you said you lost a good job."

*Tread lightly and try to remember exactly what you told him,* she advised herself. "I...said I found out that nothing was secure. Which is true. And when I did, Hilly and I decided on a lark to..." *Use the explanation Hilly always gives.* "To see the country and take advantage of a time in our lives when neither of us have any ties to hold us back."

"Then you could have stayed where you were and found another job?"

She shrugged. "I imagine so. I didn't try." Mitch bit her bottom lip, watching him look out at the dancers as if he were weighing what she said. She decided to use the pause to change the subject. "So, speaking of jobs, how long has your secretary worked for you?"

He looked back at her. "My secretary?"

"You know, the gorgeous woman who couldn't leave you alone this afternoon."

That made him laugh. "You sound jealous. Could that be?" he teased.

She hadn't meant to seem that way. But if it got her off the hook of the other conversation then it was worth it. She feigned innocence. "Jealous? Who me?"

She could tell by his expression that he hadn't forgotten what they had been talking about before. But he seemed to decide to yield to her desire to take it no further. "Nora has worked for me for about a year."

"Only a year," she mused. "From the way she acted I thought she had been with you longer than that."

"It's *only* a business relationship."

"Is it?"

"Would you care if it wasn't?"

"Yes." She had intended for that last word to sound as flirty as the rest, but instead it came out sounding like the truth.

He looked directly into her eyes and smiled a genuine smile that answered her unwitting honesty. "I'm glad."

Just then Hilly and Alfred came back to the table and interrupted the moment, followed closely by the observant waiter who reappeared to uncork and pour champagne.

After Alfred's toast to Hilly, Patrick led Mitch to the dance floor. The song being played was a slow one. Patrick held her close. He kept her hand in his against his chest, the other on her bare back. It hadn't occurred to Mitch when she dressed that the low dip of the sequined top would expose her to his touch, otherwise she might not have worn it. As it was, the feel of his hand on her skin, big and warm, his thumb smoothing up and down, made her forget herself. She melded into him but managed to swallow the instant rise of desire to say, "I don't think you've told me—have you ever been married?"

He laid his cheek against her temple. "I came close once."

"How close?"

"I was considering how to pop the question."

"But you didn't?"

"No, I didn't."

"Cold feet?"

He arched back and looked down at her. "Don't confuse me with those commitmentphobic men in our generation who are giving the rest of us bad reputations. Marriage doesn't scare me."

The music was relaxing and being held in his arms bolstered her courage enough to pursue this. "Then why didn't you ask her to marry you?"

"I found out in the nick of time that it was a blank check she wanted and not me."

She must have been out of her mind. "I'm sorry," she said even though she wasn't. If he had married the other woman, Mitch wouldn't have been there with him at that moment. "Were you hurt by it?"

He seemed to think about that. "I was hurt, but more than that I was damn mad at being used and lied to."

Had that really been as pointed as it sounded? Or was it just her own guilty conscience at having lied to him herself? Mitch chose the guilty conscience explanation because it was less unnerving. She changed the subject. "Well, I can't even say I've been close to getting married. Just keeping up with Hilly has left me a lap behind most of the time."

"Your grandmother."

"Yes," she answered a little cautiously because his response had sounded oddly pointed, too.

"That hardly seems fair. You should have a life of your own."

"I haven't minded."

"I don't think I've ever met anyone who's so close to a *grandparent*."

No, she was definitely not imagining things. There was an undercurrent in his voice. Still, she tried to make light of it. "But you have to consider if you've ever met anyone quite like Hilly."

"No, I can't say I ever have."

The music ended. Keeping a hold of her hand, Patrick took her back to their table just as Hilly was exclaiming to Alfred that she had tasted better lobster only last year when she and Mitch were in Seattle.

"Seattle?" Patrick repeated as a question to Mitch.

"We spent a few months there," she told him without expounding.

"How many places have you been in the past three years?" Patrick asked.

It was Hilly who answered with her usual vigor. "Let's see. Besides Seattle, there was Boston, Kansas City, Los Angeles, Phoenix, Santa Fe and Cheyenne. After we decided to see the country we just went wherever the urge took us."

"Well, there won't be any more of that," Alfred proclaimed as he got up and pulled Hilly with him to jitterbug.

"That's quite a list for only three years," Patrick said when the older couple had gone. He began tracing the rim of his champagne glass with his thumb.

Again he seemed to be saying more than his words conveyed. Mitch frowned at him and decided to attack this head-on. "Is there something bothering you tonight?"

His glance dropped to the glass. His hesitation seemed ominous to Mitch. Her mind ran through a list of things that might have been said that exposed something in her past.

Before she could come up with anything he dipped his thumb into the bubbly drink and brought it to her mouth, his other fingers curving under her chin. He traced her lips with the champagne and smiled in a way that made her think he was conceding something. "Tonight it doesn't matter," he told her finally. "We're out for the first time, without a struggle, for an evening of pure enjoyment. That's all that makes any difference."

It wasn't altogether reassuring, but rather than push something that had the earmarks of being unpleasant and possibly dangerous to her, Mitch merely returned his smile.

At that moment the jitterbug ended and another slow song started. Patrick removed his hand and winked at her. "Didn't we come here to dance?"

Mitch hesitated for only an instant, reminding herself that this evening was an island unto itself. Then she smiled and took his outstretched hand. "I think that was the idea."

It was nearly two in the morning by the time they got back to Alfred's house. The older couple were showing their age; fatigue was making them move more slowly than usual. "I'll let Patrick out the back and lock up. You two go on to bed," Mitch said once the four of them were inside.

The remainder of the evening had been unmarred by whatever had been troubling Patrick. Mitch couldn't remember ever having had a better time. It occurred to her that she knew why dancing had been invented—it gave two people an acceptable excuse to hold each other when anything more intimate wasn't appropriate.

"You did want to go out the back, didn't you?" she asked Patrick after Hilly and Alfred had said goodnight and headed up the stairs. "I just assumed since that's the way you come and go most of the time."

His smile was slow and showed no sign of his earlier mood. "That's fine."

Only two lights were on—the one in the foyer and a lamp in the living room that turned on automatically after dark. Mitch didn't bother with any more as she led the way through the kitchen to the back door. But rather than merely letting Patrick out she stepped onto the patio ahead of him. For the first time in days the night air was cooled by a slight breeze and it felt good after an evening of dancing.

"Tonight was so nice," she told him by way of thanks. She slipped her shoes off and went to the edge of the pool to drag her toe through the water.

"It was good for me, too," he said, following her.

Mitch looked up from the water to find him making no move to go home.

"We could end it with a swim," he suggested.

"It's awfully late," she observed without much conviction because the idea was appealing. "I don't think I have enough energy left to do anything but float, anyway."

"Floating is good enough. I'll be back in five minutes," he said, making the decision for them both.

She thought of calling after him to tell him no, but somehow the word just didn't come out of her mouth. It was late and she was tired, but in a way she felt as if she had had only half the evening with him and she was loath to have it end now when he was back to normal. Instead she ducked into the laundry room where her black tank suit, washed that morning, had been hung to dry. She shed her evening clothes and pulled it on.

Patrick wasn't back yet when she eased down the steps of the kidney-shaped pool. The water was smooth and just cool enough against her skin. She felt strangely weighted and weightless at once, tired from all the dancing and the late hour, and yet buoyed by the water. With her feet on the bottom she let just her arms float to the surface, laid her head back and closed her eyes. It was strange but the feel of Patrick's arms around her as they had danced was as vivid as if he were there with her.

Then she heard the creak of the gate. Only moonlight illuminated his tall, lean form as he came near but she could see enough to know he was wearing dark swimming trunks rather than those yellow shorts she'd seen before. It was slightly disappointing.

He dived in and a moment later surfaced directly in front of her. "Hello, lady," he greeted in a quiet, husky voice that seemed to echo the way she felt.

"Is this a swimming pool pickup?" she joked, surprised to find her own voice much the same.

"Well, you do owe me a good-night kiss."

"It was a good night," she allowed lazily and then wrinkled her nose at him. "But you're all wet."

"I can fix that." Before Mitch knew what he was doing he had scooped her off her feet, into his arms and swung her like a pendulum until her face and hair were as wet as his. Then he set her back on the pool bottom.

"That was a dirty trick," she told him with a laugh, smoothing her hair back with both hands.

"It's like eating garlic—as long as we both do the same thing one cancels out the other."

"It was still a dirty trick."

"Maybe it'll be worth it." His tone was heavy with insinuation as both of his hands closed around her shoulders. He drew her to him and his mouth came down onto hers.

There was some familiarity in his kiss now, and yet the urgency in it was new. His lips opened and his tongue was more insistent than it had ever been before. But Mitch understood because she, too, was feeling a need greater than what she'd felt the other times he had kissed her. She answered the thrust of his tongue with her own; her mouth opened as wide as his.

Instant fire lit inside of her to burn away the lethargy of moments earlier. She slid her hands up the mountains of his biceps, across the straightness of his shoulders, finding a place for one to stop on his thick, corded nape and the other on the tendons of his back. In her mind's eye was the image of how he had looked when she had watched him swim that Saturday morning, and it heightened the sensation of touching him now.

His arms wrapped around her and held her closer still. When his hands began a slow rise from her waist to the sides of her breasts she drew a quick, deep breath of anticipation, willing him to hurry. His fingers found a way underneath her suit, barely reaching the nipples that craved his touch.

Glorious sensations coursed through her. Every nerve seemed exposed on the surface of her skin. Her stomach fluttered and there was a kind of itch between her legs that reminded her just how much woman she was in response to how much man he was, letting her forget everything else.

His mouth left hers and he half kissed, half nibbled his way down her chin, the soft, sensitive area behind, down the rise of her throat into the hollow. Maybe he could reach with his lips what he hadn't with his fingers....

The buoyancy of the water made it easy for her to lift herself up slightly higher so his mouth could work magic across her collarbone. But instead of going lower, he went back to the dip where her neck curved into her shoulder.

"Tell me your secrets, Mitch," he whispered raggedly.

The fires inside of her were instantly extinguished as reality reared its ugly head. Mitch swallowed disappointed desire. She drew her head up straight and sunk back into the water. "Is that what was on your mind tonight?"

His silence was confirmation enough.

Mitch pushed away from him. "Secrets are meant to be kept," she said quietly and yet with a firmness and finality that were unbreachable. "Good night, Patrick."

Without another glance at him she found her way back to the pool stairs and climbed out, leaving with all the dignity she could muster when her body was still demanding so much more.

## Chapter Six

As Mitch poured herself a glass of orange juice the next morning she wondered how a house like this could have such thin walls. The sounds of Hilly and Alfred's reunion had awakened her early this morning and were still coming from the sauna in the master bedroom.

Mitch glanced at the clock on the stove. She was already late for her appointment to take the hearse in for new brakes and it didn't seem as though Alfred had remembered that he was supposed to follow her so he could bring her back home after she left the car with the mechanic.

Hilly's laughter carried down to Mitch as clearly as if she was in the same room. It made Mitch cringe. She didn't begrudge the older couple any of the pleasure they found in each other. It was just that it felt like an invasion of their privacy for her to be hearing it. And she needed to get the car in. If Patrick hadn't gone to work yet maybe he would follow her.

The thought of him made her stomach do a somersault and the fact that she had enough feelings for him to cause it wasn't the reason. She had been up most of the night before wondering what he knew. *Tell me your secrets,* he had said, and the words had been a litany repeating themselves over and over in her head ever since.

What *could* he know?

Nothing, had to be the answer. Or at least she couldn't think of anything. Had Hilly said something to cause him to ask such a thing? She doubted it. Even when Hilly made a slip she was so adept at covering it up or explaining it away that Mitch didn't believe that could be the cause.

Maybe it had been a metaphor. Maybe he didn't mean literal secrets, but figurative ones, like what made her tick. But his strange mood earlier in the evening didn't seem to support that.

Mitch took a sip of her orange juice. This time it was Alfred's laugh that interrupted her thoughts and she glanced at the clock again. She really had to get the car in and Patrick was her best bet.

If there was something he knew, she decided, it was better to find out than to sit and wonder. Not that she would raise any more suspicions by asking straight out. But avoiding him wouldn't tell her anything and it would only make him all the more curious. No, the best thing to do now was to face him exactly as she would have before he'd said it.

With the image of his early-morning swim in mind and not wanting to walk in on a rerun of it by going through the gate in the hedge, Mitch went out through the front to Patrick's carved door. She rang the bell and waited. *Please don't let him know anything.*

"Mitch," he said in surprise when he opened the door.

He wore only those same yellow tennis shorts and even though they were dry now, in Mitch's mind's eye they were wet, clinging and nearly transparent. She swallowed and looked over at the pink hearse parked along the curb. "I have to take my car in for some work. Alfred was going to follow me but—" she had to clear her throat "—he and Hilly are...otherwise occupied. I wondered if you might have the time before you go in to your office?"

"I'm working from home today. But I'd be happy to anyway."

She couldn't very well keep looking at her car when he answered her, so she concentrated on keeping her eyes on his face when she turned back to him. "Great. I'd really appreciate it. It's that first service station on the right as you go down Bowles toward Santa Fe. I'm going to leave now because I'm late as it is. You can pick me up when you're ready." She turned to rush off but he grabbed her arm and stopped her.

"It'll only take me five minutes to get my keys."

He pulled her inside and Mitch had no choice but to wait. She managed to keep her eyes off his derriere, but the span of his bare shoulders and his tan, V-shaped back didn't do much toward easing her overstrained senses.

"Weren't you supposed to start that research job Al got you with his writer friend today?" he asked from down the hallway that led to the kitchen.

Mitch clasped her hands behind her back and stared down from her white T-shirt and jeans to her tennis shoes. "No, tomorrow," she called.

The slap of his sandals against the floor announced that he was back, and Mitch looked up. He had slipped on a black tank top that accentuated his well-developed pectorals. He was saying something and she realized suddenly that she didn't know what. "I'm sorry, I didn't hear that."

"I said what are you going to do with your day?"

Shrugging, she stepped back through the front door, which he pulled closed after them. She glanced at Alfred's house. "Maybe they'll be worn out by the time I get back," she muttered before realizing that she was voicing her thoughts rather than answering Patrick's question.

His laughter drew her gaze back to him. "What are they doing—running naked through the house?"

Mitch could feel color heating her cheeks. "No. Actually I'm not sure what they're doing. I just know that from the sound of things they're having a good time and I feel like an intruder. Maybe I'll work in the yard or something."

Patrick pulled one of the curls that fell from her hair clip, glanced up at the cloudless blue sky, and looked back at Mitch. "With this red hair and that pale skin I would bet that spending all day under the sun is not a wise move."

It was really not fair that such a slight touch could reignite the fires that had been alive in her last night, but there they were and all she could think was that she'd like to be whiling away today the same way Hilly was. "I'll come up with something," she managed to say in a breathy voice as she broke away from him and headed down the walk. "See you at the station."

She concentrated on her driving the whole way and forced herself not to look at the rearview mirror at Patrick. She really didn't understand herself these days, she thought, as she pulled into the service station. Why was this craving so hard to turn off? She had never had this problem before.

It took her only a minute to give the mechanic instructions and the keys. Then Mitch got in beside Patrick. It didn't help her cravings to realize the car smelled of his after-shave.

Rather than leaving the station, he stretched one arm across the back of her seat and faced her. "What would you say to my playing hooky and our spending the day together?"

"You don't have to do that. I know you have a lot of work to catch up on."

"But I'm the boss, remember? I can take time off when I want to. It'll keep you out of the sun and the lovers' nest, too. Besides, I owe you a long, lingering lunch."

Temptation. She wavered. "What would we do?"

"Anything you like."

"Something air-conditioned?"

"Museums, movies, shopping malls, you name it. We'll spend the entire day like two carefree kids and not think about anything but having a good time."

It would spare her overhearing Hilly and Alfred, she rationalized. "Well . . . I have been wanting to go to the Tattered Cover bookstore and walk around those little specialty shops in Cherry Creek."

"And eat gelato at the Riverfront Market and buy a couple of cuts of decadent filet mignon at Alfalfa's grocery store to bring home and barbecue for dinner tonight," he finished.

"How did you know?" Mitch joked, pretending he had read her thoughts.

"Great minds work alike. Are you game?"

Mitch's resistance was very low. His attitude today seemed to give credence to last night's words being more metaphoric than suspicious. With that worry eased somewhat, and knowing that the other choice was to spend the day listening to Hilly and Alfred, plus the fact that Mitch just plain wanted to be with Patrick, she gave in. "Is your secretary going to have me guillotined if she finds out?"

Patrick squeezed the back of her neck. "I wouldn't stand for it," he said with a smile.

"It's a deal then."

Mitch went home to leave Hilly a note telling the older woman where she was for the day. When she went next door, she found Patrick had changed into a baby blue polo shirt that matched his eyes and a pair of time-softened and faded jeans that fit him like surgical gloves.

They agreed to a big breakfast at the Delectable Egg before going to the multileveled Tattered Cover bookstore that looked like a turn-of-the-century library. They spent hours browsing through everything, from atlases to the children's section. Patrick bought a book on cooking for a low-cholesterol diet. "To make up tomorrow for what we do today," he told Mitch.

From there they went into a place called Chocolate Soup, thinking they were exploring a candy store only to find it was a children's boutique. Next was a kitchen shop where Patrick tried to figure out what all the gadgets were for. The snobbish sales ladies in an exclusive women's clothing shop knew him by name, and Mitch teased him about it.

"Is this where you buy all your dresses?"

He caught her around the waist and growled against her neck. "My mother calls down from Grand Lake and tells her fashion consultant what she wants. When it comes in I pick it up and either send it to her or bring it with me when I visit." Then, ignoring her protests, he bought her a red silk handkerchief.

"It's a nice thought, Patrick, but what am I going to do with it?"

He only smiled at her as he took her arm and guided her out. There he made a show of unfolding it, pinching the center, shaking it like a magician and slipping it into the breast pocket of her white T-shirt.

"For just a little panache," he said in a husky voice, which Mitch barely heard as she tried to tame the sparks that burst to life in her with only the scant, split-second brush of his fingers.

"Perfect," she managed to reply, just a little choked.

There was a poster store with a green, spike-haired salesgirl who sold him a flamingo-pink watch that he said he was going to give to Hilly. He intended to persuade her it was a more portable means of telling time than her grandfather clock. At the tobacconist shop he bought a pouch of Alfred's special blend, and when they finally did find a candy store it was Mitch who bought the jelly beans, happy to comply in feeding them to him one by one because his hands were full of packages.

The air-conditioning in the car was a welcome respite from the heat as they drove to Alfalfa's on University Boulevard. It was a grocery store specializing in organically grown produce, extra lean, specially fed beef, and everything in the way of health food. Patrick had their steaks packed in ice since they weren't going straight home. They also bought artichokes and fresh baked Italian bread.

It was mid-afternoon by the time they reached the Riverfront Market. In the plant store that took up the entire front section, Patrick wanted Mitch's opinion about a fern for his Tech Center office. When they had settled on a hearty philodendron and he had arranged to have it delivered, they went to the food court for gelato, which they took out onto the landscaped banks of the river that ran behind the market.

"So," Patrick said as they sat down on the steps to eat. "Hasn't this been better than yard work?"

"Mmm." Mitch caught a drip with her tongue before it fell off the back of her spoon. "A lot."

"I was glad to see you this morning. Surprised, but glad. I thought you might be a little...mad at me."

*No, no, don't ruin it.* "Want a bite of this? It tastes like real vanilla and real cream and it's wonderful."

He did, and then he fed her a bite of his blueberry. "So you have secrets you mean to keep," he mused then.

"Doesn't everybody?" Mitch asked theatrically.

"I don't."

"None at all?" She let her tone tell him she didn't believe it, and hoped he couldn't hear how her heart was pounding like a jackhammer.

"Well, maybe one or two," he conceded with a half-grin. "But nothing that makes any difference to anyone but me."

"Me, too."

"You don't have any secrets that make any difference to anyone but you?"

He sounded dubious and Mitch's heart beat even harder. "Nope," she answered smoothly in spite of it. But she didn't eat any more because she didn't think the gelato could pass through the tightness in her throat. Instead she stirred it intently.

"You know, you and Hilly don't look at all alike."

That seemed to be a change in subject but for some reason Mitch didn't have the feeling that it was. "No, we don't," she agreed. "Unless you consider that we both have curly hair."

When he didn't say anything to that and silence fell between them, Mitch said, "So what are your secrets?"

He didn't answer her right away. For a moment Mitch didn't know if he was going to. Then he looked at her and grinned broadly. "Secrets are meant to be kept." He stood and offered her a hand. "Come on, let's go home. Artichokes take a long time to cook."

Patrick dropped her off at the service station so she could pick up her car, and they arranged to meet back at his house in half an hour. Mitch planned a quick shower and a change of clothes.

As she passed Alfred's master bedroom, she heard snoring, and couldn't help a silent chuckle at that.

Feeling refreshed after her shower she slipped into a white sleeveless jumpsuit. It had a high stand-up collar with the armholes cut at sharp angles. As an afterthought, she took the pocket handkerchief Patrick had bought her and artfully stuffed it into the small slit pocket over her right breast. The action brought a flashback of the feelings that had washed over her when

Patrick had done the same thing before, and little goose bumps erupted on her arms.

She brushed her hair and left the long, curling mass loose to fall around her shoulders. A touch of mascara, a dusting of eye shadow, a hint of blush, just enough gloss to make her lips shine, and she was ready to tiptoe past the master bedroom and out again.

"Knock, knock," she called at Patrick's back door a few minutes later. But when he answered his voice came through the open window of the bath off his bedroom.

"Come on in. I just got out of the shower but I'll only be a few minutes. You can pour us a glass of wine."

Mitch slipped in and found the wine open and two cut-crystal glasses waiting beside it. She filled them both and then lifted the lid off the artichokes he had steaming in a pot on the stove. The aroma of garlic and olive oil wafted up.

Engrossed in savoring the cooking smells she didn't hear Patrick come in. When he kissed her bare shoulder she jumped.

"It looked so inviting that I couldn't resist," he explained by way of apology.

Mitch turned to find him looking freshly scrubbed and magnificent in black tennis shorts and a white V-neck pullover that exposed a hint of the hair on his chest.

"Any sign of Hilly and Al?" he asked as he took the steaks and led the way out to the grill where the coals were white-hot already.

Mitch brought both of their wineglasses with her. "No, but I heard snoring," she said with a smile.

Patrick laughed that deep, rich laugh of his and it sent a tingle up her spine. "Good for them. Al is really crazy about her."

"Hilly's fond of him, too." More fond than she should be, Mitch thought. Then a little voice in her head said, you have no room to talk.

"Steaks are on and everything else is ready. Would you rather eat out here or inside?"

"It's nice out here." And safer.

Patrick went into the kitchen and came back with two place settings. Mitch helped arrange them on the round glass picnic table that stood directly below his bathroom window, from which spilled the scent of his aftershave—the same scent that wafted around her every time he came near, and that tweaked something deep inside Mitch. She sat on one of the tufted chairs and crossed her legs tightly.

"I really enjoyed today," she told him, taking a sip of her wine.

"So did I." He turned the steaks and came to sit across from her. "In fact I could make a career of it."

Mitch cast a glance around at his house and yard and pool. "I don't think you'd be able to support this lifestyle that way."

His eyes met and held hers. "It might be worth it."

Mitch looked back at his house, realizing how much she liked it. Envied it. "I think what you have here is worth working for and hanging on to," she said, the softness of her voice belying how strongly she felt.

"That's a strange sentiment coming from a person who chooses to be a gypsy."

She couldn't very well refute one of her lies to tell him it hadn't been her choice, that in fact it was something she would never have chosen had she had any other option. So instead she shrugged and said, "You have a nice house."

"Sometimes it seems too big and empty. Then I realize how much more important people are than places, that without the people the places don't really matter."

Which was the real reason she had decided to become a nomad. "You sound like Hilly. 'People are what counts,' she always says."

"And what do you think?"

"I know you're both right."

"But you live in a way that doesn't let too many in, and never for very long."

"I have Hilly."

"It's a sad fact, but she won't live forever. What happens to you then?"

"I don't like to think about that."

"None of us like to think about losing someone we love. But most of us have other people in our lives to turn to, to go on with, when it does. It bothers me that you don't. Do you?"

"No, I don't. But that can't be the biggest thing in my life right now. While I have her, Hilly is."

"That's not healthy."

"Are you saying our relationship is something sick?"

"No. I'm saying that you need other relationships along with it."

Was he volunteering for the job? She couldn't ask. The answer might be one she wanted to hear. So instead she said, "Aren't those steaks about done?"

He stared at her for a while longer, then finally stood up. "I imagine they are," he said as he stepped to the barbecue.

Mitch went in for the bread and artichokes, trying hard to shake the dark, heavy feeling Patrick's words had roused in her. Losing Hilly was something she thought about, something she dreaded. It was inevitable that the loneliness and desolation Hilly had saved her from as a child would come at that time. But there really was nothing to be done about it now. When the time came she would take a different name and just hope she could live unobtrusively in one place and build other relationships.

Patrick was serving the steaks when she went back outside. "Do you ever think about settling down again?" he asked her as if their conversation hadn't been interrupted.

Never so much as here, she thought, wishing he had taken the hint and dropped it. "It crosses my mind."

"But you don't do it."

"The call of the wild," she joked. "So tell me about when you were a reporter. What did you write?"

"I get it. Cut the questions. Okay. In Grand Lake I was the only reporter so I wrote everything from crime to cooking to obituaries to the events calendar."

"And what was your favorite?"

He shrugged. "Just what I'm doing with *Probe*— championing the underdog. That's how I realized it was something I wanted to do."

"Then why didn't you move into the big city and just be that kind of reporter rather than buying the whole kit and caboodle?"

"Ego, I think. In Grand Lake I had a pretty free rein and a hand in every pie. It would have been really hard to come down here and just go to work for the *Rocky Mountain News* or the *Denver Post* as just another one of their features reporters, without even being able to input my ideas for anything else. Then, when I bought the paper in Grand Lake and reorganized it, I discov-

ered I liked the business side of it all, too. And by owning it I still got to have a say in everything." He
shrugged. "It just worked out."

An understatement. But his lack of arrogance was
part of why he was so appealing. Mitch couldn't finish
her steak and when she offered it to Patrick he took it.
She sipped her wine as he went on eating.

"What about you?" he asked between bites. "How
many different jobs have you had in the past three
years?"

Mitch screwed up her face at the thought. "I couldn't
count how many. I worked in a fish factory—the smell
was awful. I walked dogs and was the neighborhood
pooper-scooper patrol—that didn't smell much better.
I was a cleaning lady, a messenger, a doughnut maker,
a housepainter, a wallpaper hanger and the personal
assistant to some lunatic Hilly met who wanted to write
about his affair with a younger woman—as soon as I
would have an affair with him so he'd have something
to write about. I was an artist's model—always dressed,
so don't ask—and off and on Hilly and I have sold her
baked goods or her tole painting or her needlework."

"Is that all of it or just the more memorable?"

"Just the more memorable."

It was getting dark and the mosquitoes were beginning to dive at them. Patrick stood. "What do you say
to finishing our wine in the family room where I'm the
only thing that bites?"

Mitch realized as she stood that her knees were the
slightest bit wobbly and her head was more than the
slightest bit light. "I think I've had enough wine."

Between the two of them they got everything inside
on the first trip. Mitch told herself she should go home
but it was a halfhearted command and she ignored it.

She might not be able to have Patrick and his home in her life permanently but she had them for tonight and she was loath to relinquish them. So rather than protesting she led the way into the family room.

Patrick turned on a lamp only long enough to find a box of matches and light three candles in the center of the coffee table. Then he turned the lamp off.

It went through Mitch's mind to ask if he was trying to seduce her but she didn't say it. The day and evening had been wonderful and if that was what he intended... well, there was a part of her that thought maybe it was all right.

Feeling loose and, oh, so relaxed, Mitch took off her shoes and sank onto the floor against the couch. Patrick surprised her by sitting directly behind her on the sofa, one of his muscular legs alongside each of her bare arms. Rather than picking up his wineglass from the coffee table he massaged her shoulders.

He pressed a light kiss on the top of her head. "You look tired all of a sudden. Have I worn you out today?"

His hands were big and warm and strong. Mitch rolled her head until it dropped forward, freeing the way for his thumbs to smooth circles on the back of her neck. "I think it's more from the wine than the activities," she said, telling herself that she should stop this. But it felt so good she didn't want to.

"Is your life the way you want it to be, Mitch?" he asked her then, half seriously, half playfully.

"Mmm, it is right at this minute," she answered, avoiding the larger scope of his question. "What about yours?"

"This minute is pretty good for me, too," he said with a husky laugh. "But my life would be better if I knew there could be a lot more minutes like it. With you." He paused for only a moment. "I care about you, Mitch. More every day."

"I care about you, too, Patrick," she answered him, surprising herself. Even though it was true she knew she shouldn't say it. Saying it complicated things. Saying it took away her ability to deny it any longer. And then she added, "But we shouldn't," as if that would help.

"Why shouldn't we?" he inevitably asked.

But Mitch just groaned softly, lifted her head and let it fall to his bare thigh beside her.

He bent to her upturned ear and whispered, "It isn't a crime, you know."

But she denied that with the faintest shake of her head.

"No, it isn't," he reiterated as he kissed the curve of her neck.

Mitch swallowed hard. She couldn't talk now, she couldn't refute anything he said. Somehow her arm had wrapped around his calf and there was only his thigh beneath her head and his mouth on her and his breath against her bare skin. Those sensations took all the energy she had to give. They were all she wanted to pay any attention to.

He gently bit the spot he had kissed a moment before. Mitch raised a hand to his cheek. He pushed her hair back behind her ear and kissed her jawbone. Then he rolled her head slightly back and bent over to reach her lips with his. At that angle the kiss was light and chaste. In her wine-induced mood Mitch wanted much more. So when he lifted her up to his lap she went willingly.

For a moment he met her almost nose to nose. He raked both of his hands through her hair, holding her head while he seemed to search her soul with those pale blue eyes of his. Then he closed them and his mouth came over hers fully, his lips parted, his tongue urgently thrusting into hers. Mitch welcomed it with her own, her hunger for him as great and demanding as his seemed to be. She placed a hand on the side of his neck, finding a taut cord of tendon there. Her other arm curved up under his, pressing her palm into the hardness of his back while his braced her.

And then, with his mouth still in possession of hers, he laid her back on the cushions. Somehow he was lying beside her, the long length of his body partly covering hers.

Mitch slid her hand up into the silkiness of his hair, holding him to the kiss that she couldn't get enough of. She found his nape and then the side of his neck and then that small part of his chest left bare by the V of his shirt.

As if he took her actions as a clue to what she wanted, Patrick's hand came to her shoulder and traveled down her arm, his thumb slipping just inside the wide armhole to curve around the outside of her breast. A frenzy of sensations burst through her and she arched her back in invitation.

It took no more for Patrick to understand. He unfastened the single button that held her collar closed, loosening the whole bodice. Then he followed the sharpness of her collarbone outward, slipped his hand down her arm and slowly, tormentingly, brought it around until his palm cupped her breast. Shards of white-hot sparks shot from there all the way through Mitch and made a small groan rumble in her throat.

Slowly, thoroughly, he kneaded her and Mitch rocked with the ebb and flow, as if she were riding waves. Then he stopped and found her nipple with his thumb and forefinger, rolling it gently, pinching tenderly, causing an explosion of desire in Mitch, of wonderful feelings that shouted to her that this was right. That everything was right with him.

He raised his knee between her thighs and again Mitch arched her back in response. She ached to have more of him so she ran her hands down his shirtfront until she found the banded bottom and slipped her fingers underneath. His skin was warm, his stomach taut as she trailed her flattened palms upward to his own nibs, which were almost as hard as hers.

She wanted him. So much. Never had she wanted anything or anyone as badly as she wanted him at that moment.

But she couldn't have him, a voice in the back of her mind taunted in reminder. Not really. Not for long. Not forever. And if she gave in to this now, how would she ever be able to leave him when the time came?

"No." She yanked free of his kiss, turning her head away from him. He stopped instantly but the thunderous beating of her heart and the shrieking need of her body went right on.

"Why?" Patrick demanded, frustration echoing in his voice.

"No," was all she could say.

"I don't understand," he said with more control.

But at that instant, before Mitch could even think of anything to say to explain herself, a movement-detecting floodlight came on outside. It threw light into the room through a picture window. Like two guilty teenagers caught in the act, they jerked their head in that direction—and saw a man lunge away from the window and run down the lawn toward the street.

"What the hell?" Patrick leaped up and bolted out the front door just as the intruder disappeared around the curve.

All of a sudden Mitch remembered herself and bolted upright, her legs still stretched out in front of her on the couch. She pulled at her disheveled bodice, swept her hair in front of one shoulder and refastened the collar.

Patrick's voice startled her for the second time that evening. "I've about had it. I want to know what the hell is going on."

"What?" she asked dimly, glancing over her shoulder at him as he pushed the door closed none too gently and came back into the room.

He sat beside her on the edge of the couch, facing her, his arm stretched across to the sofa back. Very slowly, clearly enunciating each word he repeated, "What the hell is going on?"

There was no time for Mitch to think fast. "I don't know," was all she could manage.

His tone and the scowl on his face told her he didn't believe her. "I'd bet my life on the fact that this is exactly the same thing that happened Friday night to Hilly and that's why the police were called."

"It seems possible," Mitch agreed halfheartedly. "It must be a Peeping Tom."

Patrick's pale eyes seemed to be boring through her.

Mitch swallowed and went on to fill the silence. "Either someone is getting in past security or one of your neighbors must have a penchant for staring into other people's houses."

"Maplewood's security system is one of the best. It would take someone pretty damn determined to get past it—someone more determined than just a Peeping Tom. And as for my neighbors, this is a small, closed community. Everyone knows everyone else and has for years.''

''Maybe it's a visitor,'' she said in a hurry, before realizing the obvious.

''Like you and Hilly?''

Mitch swallowed and tried to sound affronted rather than guilty. ''What are you implying? That Friday night I was spying on Hilly and tonight she was spying on us?''

''No, that's not what I think.''

''Then what do you think?''

''Are you sure there isn't someone else who would be interested in spying on you and Hilly?''

''That's ridiculous,'' Mitch said too quickly. ''Who in the world would do that?''

''Why don't you tell me?''

''What should I tell you? Shall I make something up? All right, Hilly is the Queen of Mozambique. She left her throne for a spree among the common folk and I'm the chauffeur who drove the get-away pink hearse.'' She tried to force her voice to a more normal octave by sighing with disgust. ''I can't tell you anything.'' Then with as much dignity as Mitch could muster she pulled her legs out from under the bridge of his arm and put her shoes back on.

''You *can't* tell me anything, or you *won't* tell me anything?'' Patrick demanded.

''Didn't we play this scene last night?'' she shot at him. ''What secrets do you think I have?''

''If I knew, they wouldn't be your secrets, would they? But I do know you haven't been honest with me.''

Mitch stood, tall and straight and proud, hoping she looked insulted rather than scared. ''You're right. The Mozambique story was a lie.'' Then she headed for the back door. When he followed her out onto the patio she turned her head imperiously his way. "I can get myself home."

"With some weirdo running around here? You're not going out alone."

"Suit yourself."

The gate in the hedge creaked more loudly than usual from the force she used to swing it open. Alfred's house was brightly lit and the older couple was clearly visible sitting in the breakfast nook sharing a pizza. As Mitch went through to Alfred's yard Hilly waved to them.

"I'll be fine from here," Mitch said stiffly. She took two steps without looking Patrick's way before his voice stopped her.

"Mitch." He sighed audibly and when he spoke again there was consolation in his tone. "Dammit, I only want to help you if there's something wrong."

She held her breath. There was more wrong than he or anyone else could help with. She wanted so badly to just tell him, to give in to all the feelings she had for him and forget everything else. But she couldn't.

She exhaled slowly, feeling defeated, sad, hopeless. "There's nothing wrong," she said in a monotone.

She heard him laugh mirthlessly. "I'm here if you ever want to confide in me," he said before he left.

Mitch's eyes filled with tears. She opened them wide, staring up at the star-filled sky, and clenched her teeth to keep from crying. She had been fighting so hard for this not to happen, and yet here it was. The feelings she had for him were deep. And what a terrible time to discover it—just when she and Hilly would have to leave.

## Chapter Seven

I think it's time we get out of here," Mitch said to Hilly half an hour later that night when she finally got the older woman alone and explained what had happened at Patrick's house.

They were in Mitch's bedroom with the door closed. In her chenille bathrobe Hilly sat on Mitch's bed while Mitch paced, stopped to look out at Patrick's backyard and then paced again.

"Oh, Mitchy," Hilly sighed exaggeratedly.

"Between Friday night and this evening the signs are all there that this is the man George hired—or worse. We need to leave tomorrow morning, first thing."

"But what if it really is just a Peeping Tom as you told Patrick? Do you think they advertise themselves? Any one of the neighbors could have that predilection and nobody would know it until they were caught. Or maybe someone is going to the trouble of coming over the wall. People could be curious enough about these houses to do it," Hilly argued.

"Hilly—"

"I don't want to go," the older woman cut in.

Mitch felt like an ogre. "Oh, Hil, I know you don't. But we have to. And even if we didn't, staying here and getting closer and closer to Alfred would only make it harder when the time came."

"Too late," Hilly told her flatly.

Mitch turned away from the window for the third time and looked at the older woman. There was something in her tone that Mitch hadn't heard before. "Hil?"

Hilly shrugged fatalistically. "It's too late, Mitchy. I love the old dear. I couldn't love him any more if it was ten years from now. But there's something else, too. I'm tired. Tired of being rootless. Of moving and starting over with places and people. I like it here. I love Alfred and I feel at home in a way I haven't since we started this. I didn't even know how much I missed it until now. But here we are and I want to stay."

As much as Mitch had thought these same things about herself, and as obvious as Hilly and Alfred's feelings for each other were, it still caught her off guard to hear the elderly woman say it. And with such determination to defend it. "I understand," she said from the heart. "But you know that it just can't be. You know that if we don't run we'll be found and taken away from here anyhow. You don't want that."

Hilly sighed again and closed her eyes. "I don't know. Sometimes just the thought of having to load up the clock and go again makes the alternative attractive. At least there'd be some stability."

For the first time since Mitch had known Hilly, the woman looked her age. It was frightening. So much so that Mitch went and sat beside her on the bed and took a thin hand between her own two. "You don't mean that," she said, hoping it was true.

Hilly shook her head and looked Mitch in the eye. "No, you're right. I don't mean that the alternative is attractive. But I do mean that I just can't leave Alfred right now."

"There's too much risk, Hil," Mitch said, gently persistent. "To stay is to tempt fate. Even if the peeper isn't George's man or the authorities, there's still Patrick to consider. I told you how accusatory he was tonight. He believes the two incidents have something to do with us and he's already asked enough questions to make it clear that he's suspicious of everything else, too. The man looks for dirt under carpets for a living, for crying out loud. He's not going to stop until he gets some answers."

Hilly fanned the air with her other hand. "Even if he knew the truth I don't believe he would do us any harm with it."

"You can't know that for sure. We've lasted as long as we have by being careful and not trusting anyone."

Hilly stared at Mitch. "I trust Alfred. No, don't look at me like that. I haven't told him anything, but I would, right this very minute, without a single qualm. And I think Patrick cares enough about you to be trusted, too."

Mitch shook her head in denial but inside she was crying out to believe it. "I understand how you feel about Alfred and staying here with him—"

"You understand it because you feel the same thing about Patrick."

"The point, Hilly, is that those feelings can't be indulged. The risk is too great."

"What if I had a stroke?"

Mitch's concern was instantaneous. "What do you mean what if you had a stroke? Is something wrong?"

"No. I'm just saying, what if I did. Or a heart attack or any of the other things that can happen to a woman my age. Then we'd have to stay in one place, wouldn't we? We'd have to take the risk of being found."

That was irrefutable. "You're losing sight of what's really going on here and now."

"Not at all. I *need* to stay here now, to settle, to rest and live a real life again, even if it's only for a little while yet. Just as I would need to stay in one place until I recovered if I lost my health."

"Think of what could happen, Hil."

Hilly shook her head. "I don't want to think about that. I *need* to stay here for a while. I *need* some time with Alfred. Besides, if they'd really tracked us down why wouldn't some action have been taken by now? No one has ever gotten this close before and surely if it was George's man he would pounce rather than run off like a thief in the night. Why hasn't he brought the authorities in?"

They were all good points but Mitch didn't want to encourage her by saying that.

Suddenly Hilly's free hand covered Mitch's. She gave her one hard shake and went on earnestly. "Yes, maybe staying is a risk, but leaving now would be throwing away something worth taking the risk for. Love, Mitchy, love. For us both, because I think whether you let yourself believe it or not that's what you feel for Patrick. And that's just too rare and precious to throw away. We've earned a little of it for ourselves. It feeds the soul. Let's chance it and indulge. We'll come away the richer for it later on.''

"There's so much at stake, Hilly."

"There's so much to gain if we stay a while."

"And too much to lose if you're wrong and we've been found out."

"Let's risk it just this once. I need a heavy dose of Alfred. I need a rest."

That did Mitch in. She knew Hilly well enough to realize the elderly woman wouldn't play sick to get her own way. She might not show it, but if she said her stamina was low, Mitch believed her. The fact that her own was waning only lent strength to Hilly's admission that she was tired. But still, Mitch couldn't concede completely. The alternative was just too grave. "We'll wait a while longer, Hil, and keep our eyes open. But seriously, you know that if push comes to shove we'll have to go. There won't be a choice."

Hilly patted her hands. "I know, Mitchy, I know. But I have high hopes that everything will work out. Don't give up on us yet."

It was late Friday afternoon when Patrick took the business card out of his wallet for what must have been the thousandth time since the start of the week. James W. Gardener, Attorney at Law it said, listing a Minneapolis address and telephone number underneath. Mitch had failed to retrieve it on Monday with the rest of the contents of her spilled purse.

As he had done every single time he'd looked at the card, Patrick turned it over and read the words scrawled there. *Consider that he might be right, Mitch. If you need me, call.* Another number followed, probably the lawyer's home phone.

Patrick leaned forward and pressed a button on the intercom that linked him to Nora. When she answered he said, "See if Les is still around, would you? And if he is tell him I'd like to see him before he leaves for the day."

Then he released the button, staying stretched out across his desk before he drew up slowly, laboriously, and sat back in his chair. It wasn't fatigue that weighed him down. It was other things, not the least among them self-disgust.

What kind of a person found something that fell out of a woman's purse, and kept it? he asked himself over and over all week long. Even if it was only a business card, it was still something that belonged to Mitch. Something private. Maybe something personal.

And maybe something that could give an investigator a lead as to where she had come from and what was in her past. Patrick sighed and dropped his head to the back of his chair.

Alfred's news that Hilly wasn't Mitch's grandmother had been fresh in his mind when he'd seen the card on the kitchen floor. It had almost been a reflex to put it into his pocket. Almost. Actually he had argued with himself about whether or not to return it to her. He still could have given it back on Tuesday when they'd spent the day together. He could have slipped it into her purse. But he hadn't. And then with the Peeping Tom incident that night his suspicions had become stronger than his conscience. Not something he was proud of.

Whatever happened to blind faith, he asked himself. To trust? Where was that philosophy he'd preached as a long-haired teenage rebel so many years ago about taking people at face value, trusting in the innate goodness of everyone? It had taken a beating, that was what had happened to it. And now it was casting a shadow over a woman he cared about.

*Cared about*—a euphemism for love these days.

Did he love Mitch?

He knew the answer to that. If he didn't he wouldn't be so damn worried about what kind of secrets she was keeping about her background and relationship with Hilly, about her past, about what was going on in her life now and what kept her from giving herself up as freely as he sensed she wanted to whenever they neared intimacy. If he didn't love her he wouldn't have spent these past few days as worried about her safety as he was angry and frustrated over her not confiding in him.

So there it was. A strong chance that he was falling in love with her.

But something was up with Mitch Cuddy and Hilly Nolan. And with as deep as he—and Al—were in with these two women he had better find out what was going on with them any way he could.

With a weary sigh, Patrick stood and waited for Les, ready to put the wheels in motion.

When the doorbell rang Friday night at eight Mitch jumped a foot off the breakfast nook bench. She dropped her book and ran out into the foyer, squinting her eyes and fanning the air as she passed the den.

Before she opened the front door she very carefully peered out the curtained window beside it. It wasn't the police as she had been afraid it would be. You're really getting paranoid, Mitch, she told herself, realizing that ever since the Peeping Tom incident at Patrick's she'd thought every sound announced the arrival of the authorities.

But instead it was Patrick who stood on the small porch waiting for the door to be opened. He caught sight of Mitch spying and with a questioning expression on his face he waved at her.

Mitch let go of the curtain and opened the door just enough for her body to fit through. She slipped outside in a hurry, rapidly pulling the door closed behind her.

"Hi," she greeted Patrick a little breathlessly.

He looked down at her as if she'd gone crazy. "Is something wrong?"

"No. Everything's fine," she said a little too quickly.

"Where's Al?" he demanded in a tone that suddenly seemed accusatory.

"Inside with Hilly," she answered easily enough. "Did you need something?"

Patrick frowned down at her, up at the door and then at her again. "As a matter of fact I realized I haven't paid you for working on Monday and I came to do it now."

"Oh, good." Her throat was too dry and the word squeaked out.

Again Patrick glanced at the door, then back at Mitch. Then he sighed and said, "What the hell is going on here, anyway?"

"Nothing. What do you mean?"

"Come on, Mitch, I'm losing patience with this cloak-and-dagger mystery routine. On top of everything else that's happened since last Friday when the whole damn police department ended up here, you just peeked out the window as if you were the guard at a speakeasy and then you slithered out the door like a snake with something to hide. What's going on in there that you don't want me to know about?"

"Have you always been this suspicious about everything and everybody or am I the only one who brings it out in you?" she asked, perturbed by his tone.

"So there isn't anything going on in that house?"

"No, there isn't."

Before she could guess what he was going to do Patrick shot a hand to the knob and shoved the door open. "Let's see then, shall we?"

Mitch cringed and closed her eyes as the pungent odor of strawberry incense wafted out.

"What the hell?" Patrick headed into the silent house.

Mitch had no choice but to follow quickly behind, closing the door after them. In the doorway to the candlelit den Patrick stopped. A split-second later Mitch came up beside him and peered at Hilly and Alfred to see if the commotion she had been trying to avoid had disturbed them.

Dressed in a billowing, tie-dyed caftan, Hilly sat cross-legged on the floor, her back perfectly straight, head erect, eyes closed. She was serenely meditating. Alfred, dressed identically and sitting in the same position beside the older woman, sneaked a glance at them through one eye.

Mitch looked up at Patrick. First he seemed stunned. Then his expression erupted into a grin. She caught his eye and raised her finger to her lips to hush him before he'd even made a sound. He nodded, and she motioned him to follow her out onto the porch.

"Satisfied?" she asked, as she closed the door behind them.

Patrick's grin turned into a chuckle. "I can't wait to hear the explanation for this one."

"Meditation is Hilly's arthritis remedy. She swears by it—more of nature's way. They spent today hiking in the mountains and both overdid it so—"

"Hilly's teaching Al the cure," Patrick finished.

Mitch nodded. "And if anything disturbs her concentration she gets very peeved."

"So you were sneaking out of the house to keep that from happening. I hope all your secrets are this innocent," he said more to himself than to her.

He looked like someone who had expected the worst and been pleasantly surprised, he seemed relieved. "Does that mean you won't turn us in for holding subversive ceremonies in the suburbs?" she teased with wide-eyed exaggeration.

"I wouldn't go so far as to call it a subversive ceremony. Insanity in the suburbs, maybe."

That sobered Mitch. "Hilly is not insane."

Patrick drew back slightly. "I didn't say she was. It was a joke."

Mitch realized that a little belatedly. She sighed. "I'm sorry. I guess I tend to overreact to some of the labels put on Hilly's eccentricities."

He leaned toward her ear. "I won't tell a soul about her private arthritis cure and I assure you I wasn't calling her crazy." Then he took Mitch's arm and pulled her close to his side. "But I think I'd better take you to my house for a little wine and clear air. I can't have you going back into that strawberry-incensed lair."

It had been a long three days since she had seen him last, and Mitch had been overly aware of every minute. She had worried about the note on which they had parted, but more she had just plain missed him. The prospect of spending the evening with him, especially since he seemed to have shed his suspicions of her, was a welcome one. Except for one thing.

She pulled at the front of her tank top to sniff it. "The whole house reeks. I hate that stuff. It makes my eyes burn. Do I smell of it?"

He bent over and pressed his nose, then a quick, playful kiss to her shoulder. "You smell terrific to me."

He took her hand as naturally as if he did it every day. To Mitch it felt like reassurance that suddenly all was well between them. Rather than question it, she merely reveled in the feel of her hand in his, and gave herself over to an evening of simple pleasure in being with this man she had come to care about.

As they went into his house and headed for the kitchen he said, "How was your week?"

Miserable without you, was the first thing that popped into her mind. "It was okay. The research job wasn't for Alfred's writer friend. It was for the man's son who's doing the dissertation for his doctorate degree. I wasn't altogether sure that was allowed. It made me feel like I was being paid to take someone else's exams or something."

"Speaking of which." Patrick finished pouring two glasses of wine and handed her a check he took from the front pocket of his blue shirt.

Mitch accepted it and slipped it into her jeans pocket.

"Are you always this conscientious and concerned about doing the right thing?" he asked as he handed her a glass and then slipped a relaxed arm around her shoulders. He propelled her into the family room.

"I try to be."

When they sat down in the center of the couch they were so close together that Patrick's khaki-clad thigh ran the length of Mitch's. His arm went to the sofa back, but she was still nestled into his side. They fit together as if they had been made for each other. A strong sense of belonging came over Mitch. Belonging here in this house, with this man. For the moment she let herself enjoy it without questioning consequences.

"How about you? How was your week?" she asked.

"Long. It seems like forever since I saw you." His voice was low and rich, and he smiled down at her in a way that made her temperature rise. There was only a single lamp lighting the room but it was enough to illuminate his strikingly handsome features and the sparkle in those pale eyes.

What if she had let him make love to her the last time? she wondered suddenly, out of the blue. Would it have been such a bad thing?

She yanked her thoughts back to the present to respond to what he'd said. "I was just next door if you had wanted to see me," she reminded him with a hint of challenge.

Patrick took a drink of his wine and toyed with a long curl that fell around her shoulders. His expression sobered somewhat. "After making you mad enough to walk out on me two nights in a row I wasn't sure I was welcome."

"Who did that?" Mitch joked because she didn't know what else to say. Then she tested. "Did you find out who was peeking in your window Tuesday night?"

"No. Have any ideas?"

"None."

He watched her for a moment. "I have alerted security, though. They're tightening things up to keep it from happening anymore."

"Good."

"You mean that, don't you?"

"Of course I do. Why wouldn't I?"

Again he stared at her. Then his expression relaxed. "Innocent secrets," he murmured to himself. "There was another reason that I stayed away from you this week."

"Oh?"

"It was a test. This has all happened so fast that I wondered if I could really trust what I'm feeling for you. I thought a few days without seeing you might clear my head."

"Did it?"

"I'm not too sure," he said with a laugh. "I only know that out of sight definitely did not put you out of mind. And not only did the feelings stay, they seemed to get stronger."

Hadn't she had this same experience in the past four days? Hadn't he been on her mind constantly, even in her dreams every night? And hadn't she been trying to deny her own ever-strengthening feelings for him only to be overwhelmed by the very power of them?

"I think I may be falling in love with you, Mitch," he said then, in a tone that stated and questioned at the same time.

"I . . ." She wondered and doubted and told herself not to, but ended up with, "I think I may be falling in love with you, too."

The admission was somehow freeing, cleansing, as if facing it took some of the ominous part away. Maybe she'd lost her mind, or the wine had gone to her head, but at that moment she wasn't worried about the future, about the pain she would suffer when she had to leave him. At that moment she could only bask in the feelings.

"What are we going to do about it?" he asked in a quiet, raspy voice.

Again Mitch surprised herself. It all seemed so clear, so uncomplicated, so unthreatening. "You could make love to me."

"I could, yes," he agreed with a laugh that didn't conceal his own surprise at her statement. Then he turned more serious. "But I'd want to know it was going to be for more than just a few hours in bed."

As much as she wanted that, too, she couldn't promise it. So instead she joked, "I don't think Hilly and Alfred will miss me if I don't go home until the morning."

His hand was at her nape, his thumb feathering up into her hair. For a moment his pale blue eyes searched hers. "I believe in commitment, Mitch."

"So do I," she agreed, because she did.

It made him smile broadly, as if that pleased him even more than knowing how she felt about him. Mitch had a brief flash of conscience that she should warn him—although she wanted to commit herself to him totally, a previous commitment might force her to leave him. But before she could voice it his mouth covered hers and the well of feelings and desires that came with it washed all words away. Maybe Hilly was right and everything would work out, she thought, allowing herself the older woman's luxury of believing there was hope.

Patrick ended their kiss to set both of their glasses on the coffee table. Then he stood and, taking Mitch's hand, pulled her with him to his bedroom. A full summer moon flooded it with silvery light and he led them into a beam that fell through the window. The bed was bigger than any Mitch had ever seen before. He left her for only a split second to fling back the covers and expose shiny silk sheets. And then he was back, standing directly in front of her, a scant few inches away.

He took her head in both of his hands and tilted it up. His eyes searched her face again before he closed them and took up where they had left off in the other room. His lips were open and familiar, his tongue greeting hers.

Mitch raised her palms to his chest, finding the power in his solid pectorals. Her only thoughts were of how much she cared for this man, and how much she wanted him.

When his hands coursed up her bare arms and his fingers slipped underneath the thin straps of her tank top, tiny goose bumps erupted all along the path he had followed. He slid the straps off her shoulders and kissed his way along her jawline, down the side of her neck to her shoulder.

Following his lead, Mitch found the top button of his shirt and unfastened it. With his mouth back on hers, more hungrily now, she continued undoing his shirt, pulling it from his waistband when she was finished and sliding her hands inside and around to his back.

He wrapped his arms around her and held her close for a while, doing nothing more than kissing her, thoroughly, wonderfully. His tongue tested the edges of her teeth, teased the roof of her mouth, danced with hers, and lured it into his mouth to do the same.

Impatience was growing in Mitch. Her clothes felt like a straitjacket she wanted to shed; his seemed like a brick wall barrier. With a faint moan of yearning she trailed her hands up his chest again, and then over his shoulders, smoothing his shirt off until he released his hold on her to let it slide to the floor.

It was all the hint he needed. Rather than put his arms back around her he settled his hands on the sides of her waist, dipping his little fingers into the band of her jeans. After a moment he pulled his hands around until they met at the button. Then he unfastened it and slid her zipper down with agonizing slowness. But just when Mitch thought he was going to free her he drew his hands back up her sides to the outside swell of both breasts.

She rolled her shoulders just a little, in agony at his languid speed, and pressed her palms in a firm trail across his collarbone and down into the smattering of hair on his chest.

He chuckled deep in his throat at her mimed insistence, and answered it by caressing her breasts, then finally pulling her top down. She slid her arms around him and pulled herself up to his bare chest, her flesh to his.

Whatever amusement he had found in her impatience seemed to be replaced by a burst of urgency that matched Mitch's. Hooking his fingers in the tank top he slid it to her waist, where he caught both her jeans and her panties and finished the trek downward far enough for her to kick her clothes away. And then he shed what remained of his own.

War waged inside of Mitch. She wanted this to go slowly, to last forever, and yet she craved him so much, with such a demanding frenzy. With their mouths seeking, tasting, teasing, Patrick lowered them to the cool slipperiness of the sheets, Mitch on her back and him beside her, partly covering her, his leg riding across the juncture of hers, while his hand found her bare breast. He rolled her nipple between two fingers, gently pinched it and then left her mouth to lower his there.

He knew just the right pressure with which to nip, to pull and flick. Mitch felt as if a cord was stretched tightly through her. Her back arched as her whole body responded to him and she felt driven to fill her hands with the solid expanse of his back, the taut mounds of his biceps, the kerneled nibs of his chest.

Just when she thought he could do no more to heighten her pleasure, his palm trailed down her stomach. His hand explored and his fingers discovered that spot where Mitch's being seemed centered, only to dip inside and pull out again. Suddenly Mitch needed to feel more with her hands. There flashed into her mind the image of how he had looked floating on his back that morning she had watched him from her bedroom window, of the hair on his chest narrowing like a funnel to a single straight line that had disappeared behind the waistband of those yellow shorts. But now he wore nothing. Her hand followed the path as far as her eyes had gone. Then she paused, need and timidity arguing.

It was Patrick who settled the argument. He took her hand the rest of the way, closing hers around the long, hard shaft of him. A low groan rumbled from his throat as his mouth came back up to hers, now wide open and urgent, and his hand went back to working its own magic until Mitch thought she would burst if she didn't have all of him inside of her soon.

Then there he was, spreading her legs with a firm hand and rising just enough to lower himself back again between them. He went inside her with his body just as he had with his fingers, slowly, entering only a little, pulling out, then going a little farther in and out again until she couldn't wait any longer and raised her hips until he was deep inside her. He filled her as completely as she needed with length and thickness and warmth.

At first all he did was pulse there and kiss her again, openmouthed and demandingly. Then a faint, husky moan sounded from him, as if he were in agony at containing himself for her benefit. Mitch tightened her muscles around him, invitingly, her body telling him it was all right, she was ready.

"Ah, Mitch," he breathed, just before the first thrust. Slowly he began, his body one long, tight, controlled muscle above her. Then he moved a little faster, a little deeper, faster still, deeper still, until they raced in a perfect rhythm, meeting and parting only to meet again.

A tiny, high-pitched sound escaped from Mitch as white-hot sensation exploded within her and she clasped Patrick's back to ride with it all the way to the peak. It felt as though it might go on forever and Mitch wished it would. And then she went over the top just as Patrick's body tensed. He thrust even more deeply inside her, again and again until a final plunge held him in momentary limbo. Finally he sighed out a long breath and slowly relaxed above her.

For a short time, that was how they stayed. Then Patrick braced up on his elbows and kissed Mitch, this one soft, warm, lingering and languid. He rolled over on his back and pulled her close to his side, her head on his chest. "I think the earth moved," he joked in a raspy voice. "Did you survive it?"

"Mmm," she answered lazily, contentment in her voice.

"I mean it, Mitch, are you okay?"

"Just fine," she said in a way that told him she was much better than just fine.

"Good. Then let's have a little catnap and do it all again in about an hour."

"Okay." It was more challenge than agreement.

"I want you in my life, Mitch," he said seriously even if a little sleepily. "And I want to be in yours. Every part of it."

She didn't say anything to that. She knew what he meant. He was talking about secrets again. She couldn't tell him that she wanted him in her life, in every part of it, even though it was true, because letting him into every part of her life was something she couldn't do.

"Mitch?" he said in a near whisper, as if he thought she might be sleeping and didn't want to wake her. She didn't answer him and he finally sighed and settled into sleep himself.

Would he ever know how much she wanted to stay here with him, to love him freely and openly and honestly, forever? Maybe everything would work out, she told herself again. But somehow with passion spent, some of her ability to believe that was gone.

There wasn't anything in her life she had ever wanted more than Patrick, and suddenly an overwhelming feeling of guilt took her. Because for the first time in over three years regret and resentment, for the choice she had had to make then, reared their ugly heads.

## Chapter Eight

There was a warm body beside her, a heavy arm across her bare stomach, a mattress underneath her that was too soft and unfamiliar, and bells ringing. Where was she? Mitch thought as she began to wake up. A second later she remembered with a jolt. The warm body, heavy arm and soft mattress were Patrick's. The bells were actually the telephone ringing.

Mitch opened her eyes to early-morning sunshine streaming through the large windows beside the bed. Patrick was lying on his stomach, slightly on top of her, his head turned away and his arm pinioning her in place.

She wondered if she should answer his phone since it was on the nightstand on her side and it didn't seem to have awakened him. But somehow it seemed too...too what? Too familiar? And yet how much more familiar could two people get?

Saved by the bell, was how she thought of it when on the fifth ring Patrick raised on an elbow and reached for the phone himself. "Hello," he said in a sleep-ragged voice. Then he dropped a kiss on her lips as if they woke up this way every morning.

He turned back to the phone and said, "Hi, Hilly. Yes, she's right here with me."

Mitch heard part of the older woman's bawdy comment. She closed her eyes and grimaced. What Hilly said after that was inaudible but Patrick's brow suddenly wrinkled into confused, forlorn lines and he answered, "Well, sure, I guess, if it's so important and you insist. I, uh, think I forgot to lock the back door last night, so come on in and make coffee. We'll be out shortly."

That made Mitch open her eyes. Wide. "Hilly and Alfred are coming over here? Now?"

But instead of answering her right away, he crossed his arms on the pillow above her head and smiled lazily down at her for a contented second before he kissed her again.

"It seems so."

"Why?" It was embarrassing enough to wake up with Patrick for the first time. The last thing Mitch wanted was an audience on top of it.

"She wouldn't say. Only that it was veee-rrry important and it had to be right now."

Mitch swallowed. "What time is it, anyway?"

Patrick glanced over his arm at the clock on his nightstand. "Seven thirty-two."

Mitch groaned.

"I know." He kissed her chin. "I had plans for this morning, too."

"Plans?"

"Mmm." He kissed her shoulder, then with his nose nudged the sheet to kiss the hollow of her throat.

Mitch got the idea.

"I don't suppose—" he began.

"No, don't suppose," she said in a hurry.

He reared back and looked at her with a mock frown. "Regrets?"

That would have been a lie. Mitch smiled but she felt her lips quiver. "No," she told him quietly. "It's just that ... there's so much *light* in here this morning."

"And not so much wine in your bloodstream and you haven't had a lot of experience waking up in a man's bed."

She closed her eyes again and went back to grimacing, this time in embarrassment. "That about covers it." When he didn't say anything she opened her eyes to find him grinning at her.

"And I guess since you have everything else covered by that sheet I'm completely out of luck this morning."

"Completely," Mitch confirmed after the sound of Hilly's voice saying, "Rise and shine, you sex maniacs," carried to them from the back patio. Then she added, "Hilly has no inhibitions."

Patrick nodded. "It goes without saying."

"If we don't get out there she's liable to come in here."

"I'll take that as a warning," he said as he rolled away from her and got out of bed, as unconcerned with his nudity as he was glorious to look at.

"Coming?" he asked back over his shoulder. She had just stayed there, watching his naked backside.

"How about if you go into the bathroom and I'll dress in a jiffy?" she suggested.

"Unsightly tattoos?" he guessed.

Mitch genuinely smiled at that, grateful he was making light of her modesty. "Hundreds of them."

"When do I get to see them?"

"On a dark and windy night?"

Hilly's voice came from the kitchen now, threatening to get them out of bed herself if they didn't hurry up.

Patrick winked at Mitch. "Windy maybe, but dark won't do. We'll have to negotiate that later." Then he took clothes into the bathroom and closed the door.

By the time Mitch and Patrick went into the kitchen ten minutes later Hilly had tea steeping for her and Mitch, and was pouring coffee for the men.

"This better be good," Patrick warned in mock sternness as they all sat around the table in his dining room.

"It's better than good," Alfred assured.

Looking at the older man, Mitch thought that his lined face seemed to beam. "What's up?" she asked, trying to sound light of spirits when in fact she felt a sense of dread.

"I want to tell them," Alfred enthused. "Hilly and I are going to get married. Today. I've already called my friend Judge Thorpe and persuaded him to waive the three-day wait for the license. He's coming over this afternoon to perform the ceremony."

Mitch shot a wide-eyed expression at Hilly. Out of the corner of her eye she saw Patrick straighten and turn to Alfred with much of the same reaction.

"Hilly..."

The elderly woman waved her objection away. "Now, Mitchy, don't be a spoilsport."

"Hilly, this isn't a game," Mitch said pointedly.

"No, it isn't," Patrick put in.

The older woman sighed peevishly. "How can the two of you be so serious this early in the morning? We've come to ask you to be our witnesses."

"Think about this, Hil," Mitch said.

Alfred responded to that. "She has. We got up for an early walk this morning and I spent the whole time talking her into this. Figured once she agreed I better not let any grass grow under my feet."

Mitch stood. "Hilly, I think you and I ought to take a walk and talk this over ourselves."

Alfred answered her. "Now, Mitch, I know what's on your mind."

Had Hilly told him? Mitch wondered, silently willing him to keep it to himself if she had.

Alfred went on. "You have a place with us. Don't even think twice about it. In fact we wouldn't let you live anywhere else."

"Thank you, Alfred," she answered in a hurry before the older man said anything more, just in case. "But I still need to talk to Hilly."

Hilly put both hands down onto the table and pushed herself to her feet. "Well, I guess we'd better get to it then. There's no time to waste this morning."

The streets of Maplewood Estates were dappled with sunshine through tall maple trees. Mitch waited until she and Hilly were at the end of Patrick's driveway to say anything and then Hilly beat her to it.

"You'll never know how glad I was to go into your bedroom and find you hadn't slept there last night," she said gleefully. "It's about time you started grabbing a little gusto for yourself."

Mitch just shook her head at the comment and fell into step beside Hilly as they headed around the block. "Hilly, we have to talk about this wedding business."

"Well, it'll be a simple affair. Alfred wants to ask a few friends over. He says he knows a caterer who will do some spur-of-the-moment hors d'oeuvres. We'll have to pick out something for you and me to wear, of course. I hope that ketchup stain came out of my yellow dress."

"You can't do this, Hilly," Mitch told her solemnly.

"Now, Mitchy."

"You know you can't."

"Well, I'm going to," Hilly told her in a tone that brooked no interference. "You listen to me, Mitchy. Things are finally looking up for us. *Both* of us. We can't let the past get in the way of it."

"It'll get in the way all by itself."

"Nonsense. You don't know that for a fact."

"But it's a pretty good hunch. If not now, then later."

"All the more reason why you have to stay with me, here. Either in Alfred's house or in Patrick's."

Mitch caught the sly slant of Hilly's sparkling blue eyes. "One night doesn't mean anything."

"Ha! It most certainly does. I know you, Mitchy. You wouldn't have slept with him unless there were some strong feelings between the two of you."

"Feelings like that don't matter in view of our circumstances, Hilly."

"They're the only things that do matter. It's time you and I take what life has to offer again and quit running. Plain and simple. If I'm a serious married woman and maybe you, too—or at least involved with a rich, respected man like Patrick—well, that can only stand us in good stead. And you know that being together is our only defense.''

''And you know that none of that would make any difference.''

''No, I don't know that,'' Hilly said sternly as they rounded the block and Patrick's house came back into view. ''What I know is that I love Alfred and I'm going to spend what's left of my life with him. I also know these old bones can't go on the way you and I have for the past three years. If what we've done is going to catch up with us, then we'd better take a stand here where we have some backup.''

''Have you told Alfred?''

''No, I haven't but—''

''Then you don't know that you would have backup from him.''

''Don't doubt it for a minute. I don't. And no matter what you think, I believe you'd have it from Patrick, too.'' Hilly stopped and placed a hand on Mitch's arm. Her voice was suddenly more quiet and a bit unsteady. ''We weren't foolish to do what we did, Mitchy. But this is where it has to stop. I can't keep it up. I don't want to.''

The glisten of wetness filled the elderly woman's eyes. Only once in all the time Mitch had known Hilly had she seen her cry. It went a long way in telling her how strongly the older woman meant what she said.

''Oh, Hilly,'' Mitch breathed, enfolding the other woman in her arms.

''I'm sorry, Mitchy,'' she whispered, hugging Mitch back. ''I thought I could do it forever, but I just can't keep on running.''

For a moment Mitch didn't say anything. She didn't know what *to* say. She knew they shouldn't even stay here let alone marry and settle down. But she also knew that as hard as the past three years had been on her, they had been worse on Hilly who had left far more behind than she had.

And ultimately, no matter what Mitch thought, she couldn't force Hilly to do anything the older woman didn't want to do. She wouldn't even if she could. A show of force was what had gotten them into this in the first place. Whatever came of Hilly's decision to marry Alfred, Mitch would just have to deal with it when it happened.

She took a deep breath and straightened away from Hilly. Fear and worry and helplessness weighed her down as heavily as if they were a suit of mail but Mitch smiled in spite of it. "I guess we'd better go back and get ready for your wedding, then."

"I'd like you to call Les and see if you can get him over here for the wedding," was the first thing Alfred said to Patrick when Mitch and Hilly had left for their walk. "I already called the club and had them post an invitation to the rest of our golf buddies. Figured they could get eighteen holes in, shower and still make it in time."

Patrick had to laugh in spite of the tension he felt at the news of his old friend's imminent marriage. "Leave it to you to plan around tee time so nobody has to miss their Saturday golf game."

"Sorry, can't take the credit for that. Judge Thorpe wouldn't come this morning or we were going to have you and Mitch witness the thing in your pajamas."

Patrick went back to being serious. "Al, we need to talk about this. I don't think it's wise to rush into marrying Hilly. You hardly know her."

"Know all I need to." Alfred lit his pipe, obviously unconcerned.

"That's what I thought about Amy, too. In fact that's what you thought about her when you introduced us. If it hadn't been for your friend putting a bug in your ear about her past and what kind of woman she was, where would I be now?"

Alfred looked up at him with an amused frown. "You think my Hilly is a gold digger?"

"It isn't that, necessarily, no. But I do have some questions about both Mitch and Hilly that make me think the two of us should be just a little cautious. Jumping into a marriage is anything but."

"I'm surprised at you, Pat. You took that girl to bed with you all the while thinking she's up to no good?"

"I care about her, Al. As much as you must care about Hilly. But I think you and I both had better not let those feelings rule until we get some answers."

Alfred made a disdainful face at that. "I don't have any questions."

"Well, you should. Like where did these women come from originally? Why have they lived like gypsies for over three years? Why do they pass themselves off as grandmother and granddaughter when they aren't even related? Why are two intelligent, obviously well-educated women without so much as a job or a pension between them? And what about Hilly's clock and the clothes they wore the night we went dancing? That clock is worth a small fortune and if either of their outfits that night came in with a price tag of under two thousand I'll eat my hat. Why do two people who subsist on an income from odd jobs, who don't even have a place to live, have belongings like that? Why are they so ready to stay in other people's houses? To accept the hospitality of wealthy men Hilly scouts funerals to find? The list goes on and on and I don't think you have any more answers than I do."

The older man shrugged. "I don't care."

"You better care." Patrick took a breath and tried to hang on to his patience. He hadn't realized himself just how many suspicions he had about Mitch and Hilly until he had begun to list them for Alfred. He also hadn't realized how damning that list sounded.

He sighed and looked his neighbor directly in the eye. "Just put the wedding off for a week, Al. That's all. Give me some time to see what I can find out about them."

"I don't like the sound of that, Pat."

"I'm not any happier about it than you are. But dammit, Al, it isn't as if these two women have led ordinary lives with roots and backgrounds that are an open book."

Alfred seemed to think about that for a moment. Then he shook his head. "It doesn't matter to me," he reiterated. "Listen, Pat, for you maybe caution is a good thing. You have so much of your life ahead of you. I know how bad it could have been if you had married Amy. If she had gone so far as to have a couple of kids, she would have taken you for everything she could get and then some. She would have tied up your whole future—emotionally and financially—in knots."

"What makes you think you aren't facing the same risk?"

Alfred waved that reasoning away with one of Hilly's gestures. "I'm nearly eighty years old. How much longer do I have left? Even if Hilly was only marrying me for my money—which I don't believe—but even if she was, so what? It isn't as if I have my life savings in coffee cans buried in the backyard that she could dig up, walk away with and leave me penniless. Besides, I want to see her have the best." He shook his head again and finished, "If marrying Hilly is reckless, well, hell, so be it. If you can't be reckless at the end of your life, when can you? I love her. She puts the spark back in my plugs. Seems to me that Mitch has done that same thing for you."

"Just a week, Al. Just wait a damn week."

"We love each other. That isn't something anyone at any age should ignore. At my age a week could mean I won't live to see it. No, sir, I won't wait." The older man leaned forward and pointed at Patrick. "If I were you I'd stop being so damn suspicious. These are both good women. I know it, no matter how things seem. And you'll be almighty sorry if you lose Mitch because you're doubting her and snooping around into things that are over and done with."

Patrick shook his head in denial. "Where would I be if I had followed that advice with Amy?"

The wedding was at three that afternoon. Judge Thorpe took his place in front of the fireplace in Alfred's living room. To his left stood Alfred and Patrick.

As he watched the bride approach her groom, it didn't surprise Patrick that what Hilly wore was unconventional. Her gown was a nearly fluorescent yellow sundress, she had sandals on her feet, and a green scarf tied like a sweatband around her head, trailing a long tail down over her right shoulder. It also didn't strike him as odd that rather than coming in alone or on the arm of a man, she was given away by Mitch. Hilly's eccentricities were just a part of her. But unlike before, they didn't seem amusing to Patrick. In fact, Patrick's mood would have been more appropriate for a funeral. And if the expression on Mitch's face was any indication, he wasn't the only one in the room feeling less than joyous.

Mitch wore a silver-gray suit. The jacket had no lapels but was an uninterrupted V over a white blouse with a cowl neckline. The pants that matched were slim, straight and sharply creased, and all together the outfit added yet another question to Patrick's list—it was obviously of higher quality than what was worn by most upper-level women executives he had encountered.

As Hilly and Alfred took their places in front of the judge Patrick moved a step away and turned just enough to look at Mitch. He barely heard the words of the ceremony. Instead he studied the curly-headed woman he had fallen in love with.

Staring down at the floor, Mitch seemed lost in thought. She looked troubled and that puzzled him. If this was all part of some devious plan to swindle Alfred, or just to live off of him, why wouldn't she be elated? Or at least satisfied? Instead her expression was full of worry. He had the sense that she was withdrawing into herself, almost as if she really was giving Hilly away and now had to go on alone.

Seeing it clenched a knot around his heart and Patrick wanted to comfort her, to tell her he was there for her. He even willed her to look up at him so he could reassure her with a smile, but she never did.

What if everything in her past, everything he was suspicious of, was innocent? What if the only thing causing her secrecy was nothing but pride or embarrassment at her situation and circumstances? It was possible. Hadn't that been his initial impression, after all? That her pride was what kept her from elaborating on the details of some bad luck? Maybe that impression had been the right one and his own past was what raised the other, ugly doubts. Patrick wanted to believe it. In fact he was inclined to.

Maybe, he told himself, it was time for some plain, straight talk. No allusions to secrets. No questions cloaked in passing conversational curiosity. Because if the look on her face was any indication, she was struggling with a decision that didn't make her happy and Patrick was worried that that decision might just be about whether or not to leave here without Hilly.

The judge pronounced Alfred and Hilly husband and wife. They kissed long and hard, then turned to their guests. Patrick and Mitch were left standing face-to-face behind them. He took a step toward her but that was as far as he got before Les Burns weaved his way through the other guests and stopped him with a hand on his arm.

"I need to talk to you."

But before Patrick could either listen to Les or reach Mitch, Hilly and Alfred seemed to remember their attendants. Both turned to draw them into the makeshift receiving line.

The half hour Patrick spent greeting wedding guests seemed like years. He itched to get Mitch alone and talk to her. When everyone had said their congratulations and the party began moving into the dining room where coffee, champagne and food were being served, Patrick finally made his way to her. There was such sadness in her eyes when she looked up at him that he wanted to wrap his arms around her and comfort her. But instead he took her hand and said, "Come on," as he pulled her with him to the den.

"Hi, remember me? The next-door neighbor?" He tried to lighten her mood as he closed the door behind them.

Mitch turned to him, smiling a bit wanly. "Vaguely. Are you the one who swims early in the morning in a pair of yellow shorts that a person can see right through when they're wet?"

That confused him. "I don't know. Am I?" he asked as he led her to the sofa.

Mitch sat there and Patrick perched on the coffee table directly in front of her, still holding her hand. Her smile turned more genuine. "I think so. And you should be more careful. My bedroom looks right out over your pool."

"Did you enjoy it?" he teased her with a lascivious tone, happy that her spirits seemed to be lifting with the banter.

"As a matter of fact I felt so guilty for watching that I almost didn't."

"Almost."

"Almost," she confirmed, picking a piece of lint off his blue pin-stripe suit. "We really shouldn't be in here, you know. How will it look for the best man and maid of honor to desert the celebration?"

He captured her other hand. "You looked like you needed to desert it."

"I did?"

"Mmm. I don't think I've ever seen anyone look so miserable at a wedding."

"Miserable? I'm not miserable."

"What are you then? Certainly not happy."

Mitch shrugged and glanced past him. "I am happy for them," she obviously hedged.

"Somehow that sounded as if it should be followed with a 'but.'"

"I just think they may have been a little impulsive, that's all."

Patrick nodded his agreement, staring at her until she met his eyes again. "What happens now?"

"I think we eat wedding cake."

"You know that isn't what I mean. What happens to your future now that your traveling companion is married and settled down? Al told me the day he got home from his golf tournament that Hilly was putting this off because of you. I couldn't help feeling that some of your dark mood was from worrying about that yourself."

Again she shrugged it off. "Oh, I don't know. This has all happened so fast I haven't really had time to think about it."

Patrick let a moment pass while he studied her. "I love you, Mitch," he told her then. "And I decided during that ceremony that it's time we confront some things."

Her hands in his tensed. But she didn't say anything, so he continued.

"I know there's something going on with you and Hilly and I want you to tell me what it is."

For a moment she seemed on the verge of doing just that. But then she said theatrically, "What do you think? That we're notorious bank robbers on the run?"

"Are you?"

"Patrick," she chastised as if it were absurd, but didn't elaborate or directly refute it.

It suddenly occurred to him that she did a lot of that—divert with humor, or answer a question with another question, or just let something hang and change the subject. It didn't seem as if she ever really lied to him outright, and that fact made him the most suspicious. If she told outright lies about her past they would have been harder to spot. As it was he gave her points for not being a liar at least, but it only provoked more suspicion in him.

He sighed and repeated, "I know there's something going on and I want you to tell me what it is. I'll be honest with you—because of my own past experience I couldn't help thinking you and Hilly might be gold diggers."

"Gold diggers?" she parroted with astonishment.

"Odd jobs don't pay much, you don't have a place to live, you said yourself that house-sitting was one of the things you did often. All that could be translated into living off of other people."

He saw her pride rise with her shoulders. "When we house-sit we perform a service. In exchange for our taking care of things we have a place to stay. Beyond that, we don't eat anyone's food, or take advantage of anything we find in their home, and with the exception of Alfred, we always leave when they return. Neither Hilly nor I are gold diggers."

"I know." As he said it he realized suddenly how clearly he really did know it. "But I'm just as sure that there's something else you're hiding. I don't know why and whether it's from pride or shame or fear, but I know there's something. And I can't imagine that you could have done anything so wrong that I can't hear about it."

She pulled her hands out of his. "I haven't done anything wrong."

"Good. Then tell me what it is that makes you so secretive."

For the second time she looked tempted to confide in him.

"I love you, Mitch," he said to encourage her. "You can tell me anything."

He felt as if she were sizing him up, as if there were some argument going on inside of her. But then she seemed to sag. She shook her head and again couldn't look him in the eye. "You're imagining things."

It was frustrating to feel so close to finally finding out and then have her pull back. "Dammit, Mitch, I love you," he said as if that were reason enough.

"I love you, too," she answered in a quiet tone that seemed more a lament than a declaration.

"Then talk to me. Tell me what the hell is happening with you. Let me help you. I know that Hilly isn't—"

Just then the door opened and Les poked his head into the den. "Al said you were in here."

"Not now, Les." Patrick's impatience echoed in the tension-filled air.

But Les's expression was grave, his tone insistent. "Now is exactly when it has to be. We need to talk, Patrick."

Mitch seized the avenue of escape, bolting to her feet. "I'll leave you two alone," she said as she hurried out.

"Damn," Patrick breathed to himself, shaking his head. Then to his friend he said, "This had better be good."

"Important, it is. Good, it isn't." Les closed the door and moved to stand behind one of the chairs. "I had a call from our investigator just before I left this afternoon."

"Alabama fell through," Patrick guessed in a clipped tone that told his friend how irritated he was at being interrupted for this.

"Alabama fell through yesterday. I was saving that until Monday so I wouldn't ruin your weekend. It can still keep until later. What I came in here to tell you now won't."

Patrick stared at Les and waited.

"The investigator who's looking into Mitch's background called me today. I wanted to let you know what he found before you got caught up in wedding romanticism and—"

Patrick cut him off. "What did he find out?"

Les looked at him from beneath a dark, ominous scowl. "He called the lawyer on that business card you gave me. The man wasn't willing to answer questions. The only thing he said was to relay the message to Mitch that she would be better off turning herself in than waiting to be arrested."

Patrick cursed. He closed his eyes, sighed and shook his head. He really hadn't believed it was something this bad. "Is there more?"

"No. The investigator doesn't know what she's wanted for and he won't be able to find out until Monday."

"Was there any mention of Hilly?"

"I thought this was just a background check on Mitch?"

"It was. But I wondered if Hilly had been included in that message."

"Not the way it was relayed to me." When Patrick didn't say anything Les suggested, "Maybe it's something small or ridiculous or trumped up or—"

"Or not."

"I'm sorry, Patrick," Les muttered.

"Yeah. Me, too." He took a deep breath and stood. "And I'd say it's past time for the truth."

## Chapter Nine

I know Hilly isn't your grandmother."

Mitch had busied herself emptying ashtrays the moment Hilly, Alfred and Patrick headed to the front door to see the last guest out. She was hoping Patrick would leave, too, but instead his voice came from behind her as she stood beside the trash compactor.

It took her a moment to realize she was frozen halfway to dumping the last of the ashes into the bin. She finished, closed the compactor and started to wash the ashtrays before she answered him, forcing herself to sound calm when she felt anything but.

"How did you find out?"

"I've known since the day Al came back from his golf tournament. He said he had *assumed* that was your relationship, too. But Hilly had set him straight."

Mitch nodded and went on washing ashtrays.

"I also know you're wanted in the State of Minnesota."

This time Mitch stopped breathing. It took her a moment to remember to start again. "When did you find that out?"

"Just this afternoon. What the hell is going on, Mitch?"

She bought herself some time by answering the more innocuous part of the question. "When I came home and found the police here that first night I could hardly march into the middle of it and ask if they were looking for me, could I? I knew that a lot of older people own houses in Maplewood Estates and saying I was visiting grandparents just popped into my head."

"So I hadn't misunderstood. Hilly just took it up where you left off. That was also why your car was parked so far away and you came from the opposite direction, wasn't it?" Anger made his voice crescendo.

Mitch merely nodded her confirmation as if washing ashtrays were more important.

He reached around her and turned the water off with a vengeance. "Dammit, stop that and talk to me."

She took a deep breath and held it for a moment as if it would give her strength. Then she dried her hands methodically and turned around to face him. His expression was an illustration of disillusionment and it stabbed her.

"Now tell me what you're wanted for," he demanded.

"She kidnapped me," Hilly said from the doorway, where she appeared suddenly with Alfred right beside her.

"What?" Patrick nearly shouted.

"I said," Hilly went on calmly, coming all the way into the kitchen, "that Mitch kidnapped me."

Alfred looked as stunned as Patrick but Hilly was her usual nonplussed self. Mitch's heart was pounding, and yet there was a certain amount of relief in knowing their secret was out.

"Hilly?" Alfred said. "Is this one of your jokes?"

"Not in the slightest," she informed him in the take-charge, businesslike voice Mitch knew well but that seemed to come as a surprise to both men. Then the older woman turned to Mitch. "It's time for us to take these guys of ours to separate corners and tell them the truth."

"Past time," Patrick put in pointedly, casting a warning glance Mitch's way.

Hilly waved a lofty, unconcerned hand. "Alfred and I will take the upstairs. It is, after all, our wedding night." Then she linked her arm through the older man's and pulled him with her. Over her shoulder she said, "Mitchy, don't spare any of it." And to Patrick she ordered, "And don't you let me down. I told her she could trust you with this." Then she winked as broadly as if it were all a game, and left.

Patrick shook his head. "Sometimes I wonder if she's all there," he commented when the elderly couple was out of earshot.

"She is," Mitch assured him confidently, slightly relieved to hear his voice missing the hostility of moments before.

But relief was short-lived when he turned a deep frown her way and said somberly, "I want to know everything. Right now."

Mitch sat on the bench seat in the breakfast nook. This was not a story she relished telling. When Patrick came to stand directly in front of her, leaning against the pantry door that faced her, his arms crossed over his chest, waiting impatiently, she knew she had to say something.

"How did you find out?" she asked, realizing that it had shaken something inside of her to be reminded of how really vulnerable to discovery they were.

Patrick didn't answer immediately. "All that matters is that I know."

"It matters to me. If you want complete honesty from this end I'd think you would be willing to give it from yours."

"Why? So you can judge what I might or might not know and lie accordingly?"

His words struck her but she met his eyes levelly. "I didn't ask you *what* you knew, just how you found out."

She watched his jaw work back and forth. He sighed and turned his head slightly to the side. "You left so damn many questions unanswered, Mitch," he said defensively.

Mitch just waited.

He paused again, obviously as reluctant to reveal his source as she was to tell him what she had confided to no one before him. Then he looked her in the eye in a way that seemed to challenge her. "The night we went dancing, when you spilled your purse and picked your things up again, you missed a business card for an attorney in Minnesota. I had one of my investigators look into it."

Mitch felt suddenly light-headed and slightly removed from herself. It seemed as if she were looking at him from a long distance and didn't quite believe what she saw. "You hired a detective to check on me?"

He didn't answer that. "The lawyer said to tell you to turn yourself in before you were arrested. He didn't say it was for kidnapping Hilly," he added dubiously.

It was as if her insides had suddenly been tied in a hard, tense knot. Whatever relief she had felt to have her secret finally out in the open was negated by the knowledge of just how suspicious he had been of her, of the fact that he had gone to such lengths. Her own disillusionment echoed in the tightness of her voice. "Well, now you know."

"Hilly hardly seems as if she's being held captive here," he said snidely.

"You must think I'm capable of anything if you'd go so far as to hire an investigator to find out for you."

"I didn't hire one especially for that. I employ several to work with the writers and reporters to check out stories for my publications." For a moment he couldn't meet her eyes. Then he shook his head and seemed to force himself. "All right, dammit. I know that's feeble. Would you please just tell me what the hell this is all about and we can argue the rest of it later."

Because she wanted the opportunity to defend herself Mitch conceded for the moment, putting her own anger and disillusionment in abeyance.

"No, Hilly is not my grandmother or any relation at all, for that matter. But she did raise me after my parents were killed. That part was the truth. We lived next door to Hilly. She and my parents were close friends. After the plane crash the only family there was were those distant cousins I told you about. They were an unsavory lot—a harridan who wanted me to play Cinderella and a lecher who found twelve-year-old girls attractive." Mitch tried to take the bitterness out of her voice.

"Sheila and David had plans to sell their own house and move into mine. The first night after the funeral I went to bed, hoping what I suspected of good old cousin David's *accidental* gropes wasn't really true. But just in case, I pushed a chair under the doorknob. A little after midnight he proved the worse of my fears by trying to come in. I climbed out the window and ran next door to Hilly." For a moment she relived the terror she had felt that night. Then she took a deep breath and finished in a stronger tone. "Hilly went to court against them and won custody. Thank God."

"And you repaid her by kidnapping her?"

"As a matter of fact, I did," she said without remorse. Then she went on defensively, "I didn't literally kidnap her. But I did take her away. Not only did I owe it to her, but I loved her too much to stand by and watch what was happening to her."

"Which was?"

"Hilly is actually Vanessa Hildegarde Nolan Halvorsen." Mitch paused a beat. "Of the Halvorsen grocery store chain. She's one of the wealthiest women in the country."

Shock replaced everything else in Patrick's expression for a moment. Then he nodded his head. "I see. That explains the expensive clothes and the heirloom clock."

"Some of the things that made you suspicious, I take it?" She couldn't help the caustic edge in her voice.

"Among other things."

Mitch went on matter-of-factly. "Hilly had . . . has a son. George Halvorsen."

"You say the name like it was the worst obscenity."

"That's what he is. Not that I would say that to Hilly. He is still her son and she might not appreciate it.

Though I can't imagine how she can think kindly of him.''

"What happened?"

Mitch took a deep breath. "George was thirty-four when Hilly took me in. A little old for mock-sibling rivalry, but that's how he acted. It was the first taste I had of his greed. His father had died not long before my parents. Having only Hilly standing between him and all that money was one thing. But he was afraid she might adopt me and he'd have to eventually share her wealth. Even after she had assured him that wouldn't happen he didn't seem to rest. I think from that time on he was determined to get his hands on everything as soon as possible just in case." There was a foul taste in Mitch's mouth that she tried to swallow before she went on.

"When I graduated from college Hilly insisted I go into the business. At the time she was president and George was vice president. She decided to retire to chairman of the board, making George acting president and me second in command."

"I'll bet George liked that."

"Oh, sure." Mitch shook her head disgustedly. "He wanted Hilly out altogether, not just from the daily workings while she still retained the power of chairman of the board, and he certainly didn't want me only one step below him. But for several years he had to live with it."

"And make your life unpleasant in the process?"

"He did his best. Of course he wanted to drive me out of the business. If he couldn't get me out by insisting that Hilly exclude me, he tried to make me opt for it. Hilly and I both knew his game and basically we ignored it. But to George my being in the thick of the business was another threat—he was sure I was going to try to take over."

"This guy sounds like a real gem."

"George is a humorless, stuffy, intolerant man. No one would ever guess him to be related to Hilly. And on top of everything else, he hated her eccentricities. They either embarrassed him, or as he saw it, cost him part of the money that he was itching to get a hold of. Five years ago Hilly funded some research into life after death and George went berserk. Then she donated a plot of valuable land to a cemetery for pets. He didn't like that any better. The straw that broke the camel's back was when she promised a million dollars to a save-the-sloths drive. That was all George could take. He was furious. He had made comments before about Hilly being better off if she let him handle financial matters. But after the sloth donation George demanded that she sign over guardianship of the estate and all its holdings, as well as give him her power of attorney."

Mitch stopped at the sound of Hilly's voice coming from upstairs. "How's it going down there? You aren't leaving anything out, are you, Mitchy?"

"Not a thing," Mitch called back.

"Well, all's well up here and we're heading to bed. Good night."

Mitch and Patrick both said good-night and then Patrick came to sit on the bench. "How come Hilly's version is so much shorter than this one?"

"There's a lot she doesn't remember," Mitch admitted reluctantly.

That seemed to confuse him but he conceded. "All right. I think I know where this is heading, but go on."

"Hilly got mad and refused. She told George she was sick and tired of his greedy behavior and if he didn't stop it she was going to disinherit him."

"Not a wise move," Patrick guessed.

"Hilly didn't know how unwise it was. A week after they'd had that fight I came home from work and found her cut, bruised and bloody."

"What?" he almost shouted the word for a second time tonight.

The memory brought all the same feelings back to Mitch—fury, outrage, horror and fear for Hilly's life. "George must have stewed over it the whole week. When he went to see her that day it was with the papers already drawn up for her to sign. Of course she refused, which only added insult to injury at that point."

"And the bastard beat her?" There was disbelief mingled with horror of his own.

"Badly. Before he was finished he told her he was going to petition for guardianship on the grounds that she was incompetent and once he won he'd put her away for good."

"And you and Hilly both believed he could do it?"

"As president of all of the Halvorsen holdings George had power, prestige and connections. In spite of her position as chairman of the board, Hilly had a reputation as a nut case. Yes, I believed it. I decided the best thing to do was hide somewhere where George couldn't find her and plan a counterattack."

"So you loaded the grandfather clock into your handy pink hearse and left?"

"I know this all sounds fantastic but it's the truth. Hilly was..." Mitch searched for the right word and settled on, "upset. The clock had been her husband's wedding gift to her. No matter what I said or did she wouldn't leave it. I was frantic and the only thing I could think of on the spur of the moment was this pink hearse I passed every day on my way to work. It was always parked outside a bar called The Urban Cowgirl. I paid a fortune to the owner to convince him to sell it to me. Taking her clock with us was the only way I could get Hilly out of the house.''

Patrick frowned. ''That still doesn't explain why you're wanted for kidnapping her.''

''This is where it gets complicated.''

''It hasn't been too simple up until now.''

''I really only meant to get Hilly out of harm's way. Once she was safe and taken care of I figured I'd contact her attorneys. But when I did I found out George had had a big head start on us. He'd been using the family lawyers—the best in Minnesota—to explore having Hilly committed. By the time I got to them they weren't altogether sure George wasn't right.''

''I see. That accounts for what was written on the back of the card. You still haven't gotten to the kidnapping charge,'' he reminded.

''This part I only know from what I read in the Minneapolis newspapers. George claimed that before he even realized his poor deranged mother had been kidnapped, I had sent him a ransom note saying if he wanted her back he would have to follow my forthcoming instructions. The newspapers said it was proven that the note had been typed on my personal typewriter, which of course George had access to since he had keys to Hilly's house. And in view of the fact that I was also missing...'' Mitch sighed and shrugged fatalistically. ''Any possibility of kidnapping is enough to bring the FBI into it. From there things snowballed.''

Mitch paused, choosing to skip a part of her story when she went on. "I didn't think Hilly was too reliable as my only defense. Who would believe anything claimed by a woman publicly known as a nut and on the verge of being declared incompetent? I was too afraid that Hilly would end up in an institution and I'd go to jail. So for more than three years we've traveled the country, one step ahead of a private investigator George hired."

"How do you know that?"

He sounded like a prosecuting attorney and it rubbed Mitch the wrong way. She stared him straight in the eye. A bit of her earlier anger seeped up to reexert itself and somehow made her feel better. "Why? Do you want to tell yours how to cover his tracks?"

Patrick's jaw clenched and unclenched. "I just wondered how sure you are that someone has been following you all this time."

"A month after it all started George raised a big stink in the press about how not enough was being done to find us. They reported that he was putting a private investigator on it. Over the years it's gotten back to us that someone's asking questions about us, or something out of the ordinary happens. We've just assumed it was the detective he hired and lived on the lookout."

"Are UFO sightings a part of that?"

Mitch explained what had actually happened.

"And the Peeping Tom at my house?" Patrick asked.

"Hilly wants to believe it's all just coincidental. I'm more leery."

"But you haven't left."

Mitch looked away from him and took a deep breath. "I've tried," she admitted quietly.

"Why haven't you succeeded?" he asked just as quietly.

"That's more complicated than this story," she hedged. "There's Alfred. There's the fact that Hilly's older and tired of running. That I'm tired of running..." She closed her eyes and wished the real reason wasn't true. But it was, and there was no escaping it. She opened her eyes and looked over at him. "And there's you."

"Then maybe, if what you say is true, it's time to fight."

"*If* what I say is true?"

This time it was Patrick who looked away. Silence fell between them for a moment, thick and tense. He seemed to be debating with himself about something. Finally he admitted, "Some questions come to mind."

"Like what?"

Again he paused, obviously reluctant to voice them and yet equally as unable to rid himself of them any other way. "Like why didn't you have a doctor's report document Hilly's abuse and go after her son with it? It could have gone a long way in substantiating your side. Surely if Hilly was that wealthy she could have brought in other counsel and psychiatrists to defend her, and she must have had some power and connections of her own. Why did you back down so easily? Why would you accept a life on the run rather than fight? Why would you let her son get away with it all by default?"

Was he playing devil's advocate? Or did he truly doubt her? "You don't believe me?"

"I didn't say that," he told her, but it took some time for him to get the words out. "I'll admit this explains a lot of things. But..." He sighed. "Call it my background as a reporter. I can't help questioning some of it. It's a pretty tall tale."

"No, it's the truth," she asserted, stung again by his obvious skepticism.

"Then why didn't you fight back? Why haven't you fought back in all of this time?" he challenged.

She breathed a derisive, mirthless laugh and consciously answered only his second question. "Do you think living the way we have for the past three years has strengthened our case? *You* think we must both be either lying or crazy to have done what we did. Is anyone else going to think differently?"

"Then why didn't you fight in the beginning?" he persisted.

"Maybe your investigator can dig it up for you."

"Or maybe you could just give me a straight answer." He sighed and seemed to concede to compassion. "It's a fair question, Mitch. Why, with so much to lose, didn't you put up a damn fight?"

The memory that answered that made her eyes fill. It was something she had never talked about before, not even to Hilly, and she wasn't quite sure why. Maybe because those first two months had scared her so badly. Maybe because there didn't seem to be a way to say it even now without it seeming to substantiate to some degree George's side of it all.

"Why, Mitch?" Patrick demanded when she didn't answer him. His tone was hard-edged again.

She wanted so much for him to believe her, to understand. For that reason she ventured it. "Because for a while she *was* crazy," she told him quietly.

It took her a moment to gather the courage to explain. When she finally did it was in a soft, confidential voice. "As soon as I found her I called her doctor.

It didn't even occur to me that he was a friend of George's or that it would matter. He patched her up and assured me she wasn't seriously hurt, but he didn't want to hear what had happened. He kept alluding to the cause as a 'fall,' saying that she was lucky she hadn't done more damage to herself. Then, just before he left he said it looked like George was right about her needing to be someplace where she could have constant supervision. To make matters worse Hilly wouldn't—or couldn't—even answer his questions about where she was hurt. After she told me what had happened she lapsed into...I don't know, some kind of trancelike state of shock. She just stared into space, and nothing brought her out of it. The doctor took it as confirmation that she was deranged and I knew it was something he would say against her if he was asked."

Mitch nervously brushed the tabletop. "I knew I had to get Hilly away from George and whatever wheels he had put into motion. But when I tried to get her to leave..." Mitch sighed. "She refused to go without the clock. She went berserk. That was when I had to go for the hearse. But even after I had it loaded she wouldn't come quietly. She started screaming that she had to wait for Mike. Mike was her husband. He'd been dead for twelve years. I had to tell her he was meeting us to get her calmed down and into the car."

Mitch swiped at her wet cheeks with the back of her hand. "I had a small cabin on a piece of isolated ground that I'd inherited from my parents. I doubted that George even knew I owned it, so I thought it was a safe place to take her. Halfway there, in the middle of a crowded street at a stoplight, she rolled her window down and started to scream that someone had killed her baby boy and she was going to make them pay. One of the people crossing called her a lunatic." Mitch's mind wandered for a moment before she summoned it back and said defensively, "I thought it was all shock. I was sure that as soon as she had a night's sleep she'd be her old self again."

"But that wasn't how it happened," Patrick guessed when, for a second time, she was lost too long in thought.

"We stayed in the cabin for two months. I kept up on what I was being accused of through the newspapers. I knew it was dangerous to be that near to the scene of my *crime*, but there was nothing I could do about it."

She looked Patrick directly in the eye. "You want to know why I didn't fight? Because even in her best moments there was no fight left in Hilly. He had hurt more than her body. And if I had fought I would have lost the battle and Hilly, too. How could I go back and say she hadn't been crazy before when she was then? She couldn't defend me and I couldn't keep her out of an institution the way she was. No matter what, I couldn't take any chance."

Mitch realized her quivering voice had risen, and lowered it. "Even after the bruises healed she wasn't well enough to be taken anywhere else. She wouldn't get out of bed. She wouldn't eat. She didn't care about anything. The most lucid things she said were about maybe actually being crazy to have raised and loved such a son, to love him still even after what he'd done. There were days on end when she drifted in and out of sleep and stared at the wall beside her bed when she was awake, not talking, not even answering when I talked to her. She had nightmares that made her scream and when she'd wake up she would be disoriented, sometimes wildly afraid and inconsolable. Sometimes she'd rant and rave, other times she'd sit in a corner and mutter to herself all day long.''

"How did she come out of it?" Patrick coaxed.

"When it was absolutely necessary I'd go into the small town that was nearby to buy groceries. I had this awful wig I wore and a pair of ugly glasses for a disguise so no one would recognize me. Anyway, we'd been there nearly two months when I overheard the store owner and another customer talking about being asked questions about Hilly and me by some stranger. I assumed George's investigator had tracked us that far. I was scared and nearly crazy myself with worry about Hilly by then and when I went back to the cabin my frustration just sort of exploded. Maybe it was shock therapy or something, but Hilly looked at me as if she had just awakened from a deep sleep and she couldn't figure out why I was acting like a raving maniac." Mitch shrugged. "That was all. She just came out of it. But by then I was afraid she might lapse back if it was all brought up again. We talked over what we should do. She agreed that with her reputation she wasn't much of a defense against George, and we decided to take life on the lam, as Hilly is fond of putting it.''

Patrick didn't say anything. His expression was unreadable. Mitch searched for a sign of acceptance from him, for belief, for support, for something positive. For anything to reassure her that to have this out in the open was not necessarily to be condemned—by him or by anyone else. But all she found was Patrick in deep thought. Doubtful thought, it seemed to her. And the emotions that had been unleashed inside Mitch while she told her story, coupled with the disappointment at Patrick's not offering ready belief in her, opened the floodgates of anger.

"What else can you find to suspect, Patrick?" she demanded caustically.

His answer didn't come readily, evidence that he didn't want to doubt her. But it was clear that he did. "It's incredible that you've been able to elude a private detective, the police and the FBI all this time."

"Is it?" she asked, hearing accusation in his voice.

He frowned so deeply his eyebrows nearly met. Rather than answer her he went on to another question. "And you aren't sure if the two incidents here are the investigator or not?"

"We're never sure. If we waited around to be sure we'd have been caught."

"It's strange that I don't remember reading anything about this. I'll grant you that three years ago I was pretty enmeshed in a sports magazine I was beginning at the time but I keep up with all the major news stories and it would have received some amount of national coverage."

It seemed clear that he was thinking out loud. And Mitch didn't like what he was thinking. "I'm sure you can look it all up in old Minnesota newspapers. Or send your investigator to Minneapolis, why don't you? Or would you like to give me a lie detector test, search my room and go through my purse yourself?"

"It isn't as if you've been faultlessly honest with me, Mitch," he defended.

"So of course I couldn't be telling you the truth now, is that it? And I suppose you think that justifies hiring an investigator to pry into my life?"

He looked as if she'd struck a raw nerve. "What else was I supposed to do? Did you trust me enough to tell me any of this freely? You say you love me but you won't confide in me."

"Even when I do you want verification. You're acting like I'm an unreliable source who needs to be grilled."

"I want to believe you, dammit. If it's all true I want to do what I can to help," he insisted through clenched teeth.

"You want to help," she repeated curtly. "Is that what you were doing when you took something that dropped out of my purse? Is that what you were doing when you sent some investigator to snoop around in my past? Were you trying to find a way to help me, Patrick, or were you trying to find out if I had something unsavory that you might not want to let tarnish you or your life? I don't think you were trying to help me. I think you were trying to protect yourself. Maybe refusing to believe me now is some warped way of continuing to protect yourself, for all I know."

"I'm trying to believe you, Mitch. But you have to admit this is all pretty farfetched. Your track record isn't too great and I've been in the news business too long not to remember a story like that."

"I see," she said in a deceptively calm voice. "George's cohorts and the law have presumed me guilty until I could prove I was innocent. Now you're doing the same thing."

"Be reasonable. It isn't as if you didn't give me cause to wonder. Now give me cause to believe you."

"In what form?"

He threw his hands up in the air and shook his head. "I don't know. God, Mitch, I want to believe you but I need some solid proof . . . something."

Her voice cracked, but still she shot back. "Where does trust come in, Patrick? Or the benefit of the doubt? But those aren't things you can lay claim to, are they? At least not for me. That's why you reacted the way you did this morning when Alfred announced he and Hilly were getting married. Did you try to talk him out of it while Hilly and I went for our walk? What did you tell him? It's all right to sleep with them, but whatever you do don't get involved in any other way until the investigation is complete? They can't be trusted until all the facts are in? Until there's solid proof?'' She spat the last words.

His silence was answer enough.

"You did, didn't you?'' she said more to herself than to him.

"That isn't how it is, Mitch. I slept with you because I love you. But I needed answers to some questions that you skirted. I thought I had an obligation to myself and to Alfred to find out what it was you were hiding.''

"And now you know, you have all your answers and you still don't believe it.'' She laughed bitterly, mirthlessly. "What will it take, Patrick? Do you want it carved in stone by a third party? Will even that be enough?'' She shook her head, doubting that anything would satisfy him. "I wonder how you'd like it if the tables were turned. If you bared your soul and I didn't buy it.''

"It isn't like that, Mitch.''

"Sorry, that's one I don't believe.'' Indignation was in full force. "I knew you were trouble that first night, but even I didn't know how suspicious you really are. Go on, Patrick, have my story verified. Don't believe it until you do. But don't expect me to be grateful for it when it comes.''

And then, hanging on tight to anger, disillusionment and more tears that pride wouldn't let him see, she walked out.

## Chapter Ten

Patrick waited for Les in the bar of the health club they both belonged to. It was quiet for a Sunday and he had already ordered two iced teas when Les hobbled in.

"I'm sorry," Patrick apologized as the stocky man painfully lowered himself into the chair on the other side of a small round table. Their racquetball game had been cut short after Patrick had hit three balls so hard they had ricocheted into Les.

"Next time work out your frustrations jogging or swimming or something that can't cause bodily harm to your opponent," Les advised.

While the waitress served them, Les joked with her. Patrick barely heard anything that was said until his friend tossed a cocktail napkin at him.

"Brooding is bad for the blood," Les told him. "So what's up that puts you on the phone early on a Sunday morning wanting to mutilate me with a little rubber ball?"

"I confronted Mitch about being wanted in Minnesota." Patrick relayed the whole story, complete with the argument that had ended the evening.

When Les had digested it all he said, "I do remember reading about the Halvorsen kidnapping. I don't recall any of the details. I just thought at the time that a big ransom was going to make food prices go up. Unless I'm mistaken, you were in England at the time chasing down Whitmore to buy out *Sports Afield*. It's no wonder you didn't read about it."

That explained it. "Then it's closer to four years ago. When Mitch said three I placed it at the time I was back here getting the magazine under way. I couldn't figure out why I drew a blank on a story that had to have hit all the papers."

"So you figured she might have made it up and let her see your doubts. Bad move."

"I know."

"What are you going to do about it?"

"That I don't know. Between doubting her and setting an investigator on her she was pretty mad."

"I'm sure. Speaking of which, shall I call off our guy?"

Instead of sleeping, Patrick had been thinking about that all night long. "No. In fact I want him to dig up everything on the situation and on the son as fast as he can."

"I thought you wanted this woman. Wouldn't you have a better chance of that if you drop this and try to trust her?"

"I want to help her," Patrick asserted hotly. "The best way to do that is to find out exactly what she's up against."

"Are you sure that isn't just a rationalization to go on with the investigation?"

Was he sure? "No," he admitted to his friend in a barely audible voice. "I'm not sure. If your memory is right and there was actually a kidnapping..." Patrick tripped over that statement, remembering that a similar one had condemned him with Mitch the night before. "You know as well as I do that any story that's been made public is fair game for someone to claim as their own."

Les nodded his head in understanding but showed no sign of judgment or of having taken offense to Patrick's *if*. After a moment's hesitation he said, "You do know that if she is who she says she is, and the story is true, it would be a great launch for *Probe*."

That thought had occurred to Patrick, too, but he wasn't sure he was ready to consider it. Instead he said, "What happened in Alabama?"

"Seems the community the old codger lived in was ready to go to bat for him, that's how we got the lead. No one who knew him for the past forty years could believe him capable of hurting anybody, let alone killing young men. But it seems that every year the guy had taken a vacation, he committed murders in other states, and then would come home to be Mr. Do-Gooder. Trouble is, he retired a year or so ago and couldn't afford the vacations anymore. He started striking in his own backyard, so to speak. That was what got him caught. His conviction was justified." Les finished his iced tea and didn't say any more.

Patrick knew what his friend was waiting for. "I don't know about using Mitch and Hilly's story to launch *Probe*. Even if it is true."

Les stood to leave. "Well, think about it. We haven't come across anything better or more tailor-made to get your baby off the ground. In the meantime I'll light a fire under our investigator in Minnesota."

"Make sure you tell him to be damn careful that he doesn't leak anything that could lead back here. I don't want Mitch put in any more jeopardy than she already is."

"No problem." Les picked up his sports bag and slung it over his shoulder. Then he stopped short. "Something just struck me. There was a guy at the wedding yesterday whom I didn't know and neither did anyone else I was with. I figured he was a friend of Mitch or Hilly, but come to think of it most of his questions were about the two of them. You don't think he could have been someone looking for them, do you?"

Patrick's hand clenched around his glass. "There weren't many people there whom I didn't know."

"Me, either, that's why this guy sticks out in my mind now. I don't think he stayed long. He came up to talk to the group I was in just after the party moved outside. I saw him kind of circulating as if he didn't know anyone. I can't remember seeing him anymore long after that."

"The wedding was a great chance to blend in with the crowd and get a closer look at Mitch and Hilly."

"Maybe you better warn them," was the last thing Les said before he left.

Patrick ordered a second iced tea but he was so preoccupied with his own thoughts that the waitress had served it and turned to leave before he remembered to thank her.

Mitch might not buy it, but there wasn't anything he wanted more than to believe every word of what she'd told him the night before. So what's stopping you, he silently goaded himself. How much corroboration does it take? Would her driver's license, fingerprints, blood tests and DNA be convincing enough?

It was one thing to play it safe, to explore questions that arose, not to charge blindly into a relationship or love. It was something else again to—how had Mitch put it?—to believe she was guilty until proven innocent. Taken that far, playing it safe was ridiculous.

So what was he going to do about it? that goading side of himself asked. It was a decision he needed to make before the investigator's report came in. Because if he could believe Mitch only with that kind of substantiation there was no hope for a future together.

But could he? What did his instincts tell him?

He had wanted to believe she hadn't done anything wrong, that whatever she was hiding was relatively innocent. He had wanted to believe her last night when she'd told him the whole story. But all along he had drowned his own desire and come up with a new list of suspicions.

Was wanting to believe her—maybe even being inclined to believe her until he could reason himself out of it—the same as instinctively believing that she wasn't actually doing anything wrong? Patrick decided that it was. Too many of his doubts had had to be bolstered with reminders of Amy and what she had done. Something that took that much effort seemed to him to be fighting natural inclinations.

He took a sip of his iced tea. It was a blow to realize how little he had trusted his instincts. How little he had trusted himself. Face it, he hadn't even trusted his best friend a few minutes earlier when Les had said he remembered the kidnapping.

Patrick had always prided himself on two things: believing in his own sense of what was at the core of people he met, and fighting against injustices. He suddenly felt as if he had betrayed himself on both counts and that made him take stock.

What did he think was at the core of Mitch and Hilly?

Hilly was unusual. She was outspoken, outlandish and uninhibited. She ate dandelions and pretended to see UFOs and wore a garish getup to get married in. She was full of life, yes. Sometimes damn odd, yes. He could see how a lot of people would misread her eccentricities as insanity.

Could she be the wealthy chairman of the board of the Halvorsen grocery store chain? She was sharp, astute, never lacking in confidence or hesitating to take control or dictate who, what, when, where and how everything was to be done. He could picture Hilly running a whole empire.

And what about Mitch? Beautiful, intelligent, perceptive Mitch. She never seemed to doubt herself, her bearing was elegant and she was as at home in sequins and silk as she was in blue jeans and sweatshirts. He had never doubted that she was well educated and had held a high-level corporate position. She was capable. In fact he had wondered how she could be satisfied with temporary, menial jobs when his impression of her on the work front was that she was as likely to take charge as Hilly was.

Certainly there was no question that she cared enough for Hilly to save her from an abusive son, even to give everything up to work odd jobs to support the older woman. Did he honestly think she was capable of doing something illegal? The woman who worried that helping research that doctoral thesis was cheating? Who had found it difficult to lie enough to convince him out of his suspicions?

No, Mitch was as upstanding as Hilly was outlandish. If anything, Mitch was too honest and had too much integrity for her own good in her present situation.

"You've really blown it, Drake," he said under his breath.

For someone who prided himself on seeing past the surface, he had failed miserably. He had let the shadow of Amy cloud his vision and he had mistrusted his own people-reading ability—that ability that had always been his own greatest asset.

And what about his goal of fighting against injustices? On that count he was guilty of perpetrating the injustice. He had refused to take her word until it was verified over and over again. She had been right, he had found her guilty until proven innocent.

Patrick paid the check. He picked up his racket and sport bag. There were four people his suspicions had affected. Hilly and Alfred didn't seem any the worse for it, but it was time to mend the damage he'd done to his relationship with Mitch.

"Sorry, Mitchy. I'd like to take your side, but you overreacted," Hilly said bluntly when Mitch explained what had happened between her and Patrick. The two women had just finished dessert Sunday night. Alfred had gone to the drugstore and it was the first time they had been alone together since the wedding the day before.

"That's easy for you to say. Alfred accepted you without knowing and then believed every word you told him. You might feel differently if you found out he had ransacked your purse, set an investigator on you and still didn't believe you even when you told him the whole thing."

"Patrick did not ransack your purse," Hilly defended him. "And actually, I was beginning to wonder if my old dear was a little senile for *not* questioning and doubting more."

Mitch smiled, in spite of feeling absolutely miserable. "I don't believe you ever thought Alfred was senile."

"Look at it through Patrick's eyes, Mitchy. I know if I were him I'd think we were suspicious characters myself. After all, there aren't too many unemployed traveling house sitters like the two of us. And we did do some lying and fast-talking. It isn't as if we were aboveboard. There were things to be suspicious of. Once anyone realizes that, it makes it hard to know when the truth is being told. Ours is a pretty incredible story coming on the heels of understandable suspicion." Hilly nodded out the window of the breakfast nook. "And don't look now but he just came through the hedge gate."

Mitch did look. She couldn't help it. She also couldn't help the fact that her heartbeat kicked up two notches at just the sight of him crossing the patio.

When Patrick reached the back door a moment later Hilly called, "Hello, Patrick. Come on in. Mitch and I were just talking about you."

"Does that mean I'm walking into a firing squad?" he asked amiably enough as he came in.

"My guns aren't loaded," Hilly assured him. "But I can't speak for everyone. Will you have a slice of alfalfa cake?"

"I'd rather have a little of Mitch's time," he said, glancing at her then.

"She has plenty of it," Hilly answered for her.

Patrick's deep-set, pale eyes met Mitch's. "I need to talk to you."

"I don't know why when you don't believe anything I say," she told him perversely, in spite of the fact that Hilly's reasoning had knocked some of the wind out of her sails.

"Mitchy," Hilly chastised.

"It's all right, Hilly," Patrick assured without taking his eyes off Mitch. "And don't take offense, but I'd like her to come home with me so we can talk alone."

"No offense taken," Hilly said hurriedly.

"Please?" he asked Mitch in a low, intimate voice.

Damn his eyes. And his angular features and his cleft chin, she thought.

Hilly waved her away before she could think of an excuse. "Go listen to what this man has to say."

"Traitor," Mitch said as she slid out of the breakfast nook with something less than enthusiasm.

Neither Mitch nor Patrick spoke as they walked to his house. Inside, she passed the wall where his niece's artwork was so prominently displayed, and walked into the family room she could so vividly picture filled with the warmth of kids and dogs and love. She wondered if he sensed how vulnerable she felt in this place and if that was why he had chosen not to stay at Alfred's. It made her anger that much harder to sustain and yet she wanted to hang on to as much of it as she could. It was a mechanism to distance herself from this man who didn't believe her even when she confided in him.

"I wanted to do this in private so if you felt like throwing things at me you could," he said as he walked over to the mantel and propped an arm there.

"I'm not much of a vase thrower," she told him levelly as she wandered over to the bookcase.

For a moment Patrick didn't say anything. Mitch stared at the titles lined up on the shelves. She could feel him watching her and she straightened her back as if it would somehow provide armor against his drawing her feelings for him back to the surface.

"I owe you an apology," he said then. "Hell, I owe myself an apology."

Mitch frowned over her shoulder at him. "I don't understand."

"I went against my own grain and because of that I did some things I'm not proud of. Things I'm damn sorry for in fact. My past isn't quite as cut-and-dried as I portrayed it, I'm afraid. It left a deeper mark than even I realized until today and made me blow everything I didn't know about you out of proportion."

"Oh?"

"I overlooked things that should have tipped me off about Amy. When I found out what she was really after it was a hell of a blow to my ego—because I didn't spot it on my own and because she wanted my money at least as much as she wanted me. I was determined that no one would ever pull the wool over my eyes again."

"So from that moment on you decided not to believe a word any woman said to you unless it was professionally investigated and verified," she finished caustically.

"No."

"What then?"

"Then you came along and took the brunt of it. You were the perfect target. Next in line, mysterious enough to fuel my suspicions..." He paused. "And inspiring stronger feelings—and as a result, more vulnerability—than she had. It all rationalized what I was doing. I wasn't proud of it, but it seemed justified when I thought about how I'd been taken in by her. Then last night when you told me the whole story I found myself incapable of believing it. I know it's probably hard for you to understand, but that was more a statement of something wrong with me than with you or what you told me. And I'm sorry for that."

Mitch closed her eyes and took a deep breath. She didn't want to love him. Every day since that first Friday night her sense that something was about to happen to force her and Hilly to leave here had grown stronger. And every day her feelings for Patrick had intensified, which would make that leave-taking so much harder. Now with Hilly loving and actually marrying Alfred, and Mitch's feelings for Patrick, everything was so complicated. If only she could sustain rage and leave him on a blaze of it, maybe it would be easier. But his explanation and apology were chipping away at her bitter resentment.

"I believe everything you've told me, Mitch," he went on when she didn't say anything. "If I had trusted my own instincts about you and accepted what I saw in you rather than pounding it down with overblown suspicions I would have realized from the start that you're actually too honest for your own good, that I could trust you. And a woman with the kind of loyalty to give up everything and live the way you have to protect someone else is a woman I want in my life."

Mitch opened her eyes and dropped her head back to stare up at the ceiling. There wasn't anything she wanted more than to be in his life. To belong here in this house with him. And yet she didn't have Hilly's optimism that it could all work out. "I just don't know, Patrick," she said very quietly, wishing for the anger back but not regaining it.

"I love you, Mitch. And I believe you."

"I love you, too. And I'm glad you finally believe me. But it doesn't change my situation."

"We can work on that. The four of us all together. What it changes is that you and Hilly don't have to face it alone."

What she wanted to think was that they wouldn't have to face it at all. That they could start new lives here with these two men and never look back. Patrick believed her, believed in her. That was enough vindication. The rest could just stay buried. But what if it didn't?

"I don't know, Patrick," she repeated. "There's always the chance that my only choice, no matter how closely we're involved or how much our lives are enmeshed, will be to run."

He came up behind her and took both of her shoulders into his hands, pulling her back against him. "Everything will be all right, Mitch. I'm sure of it."

His voice was low and soothing and confident enough for her to believe him. Or was it just that she wanted so badly for it to be true? She forced herself to warn him. "But if it isn't, you have to know that my leaving is the only alternative."

He turned her around and enfolded her in his arms, warm, powerful and protective. She rested her head against his chest, listening to the steady, strong beats of his heart. "I love you and everything will be all right," he repeated, in a lulling and soothing voice.

He pressed a kiss to the top of her head and she could feel the heat of his breath. She felt so safe that all the love she had for him swelled to the surface and made her forget to think about anything else.

He tipped her chin with a finger and looked down into her eyes. "I'll make it all right," he told her huskily just before he took her lips in a kiss that was at first soft and reassuring, but soon turned into something more.

Respite was what she found in his embrace, in his mouth on hers. There was nothing to fear, there was no past, no need for inhibitions or holding anything in check to protect herself. Nothing but wondrous sensations and a kind of freedom she didn't have anywhere else. He took her out of herself and her problems and put her in touch with only the warm velvety texture of the inside of his lips, the clean spicy scent of his aftershave, the feeling of his tongue meeting hers, and the wonderful pressure of her breasts flattened against his broad, hard chest.

He took her into his bedroom, where there was just enough light to barely see him kick off his shoes and shed his shorts and shirt. She feasted her eyes on the magnificence of his naked body as she unfastened the mauve jumpsuit she wore. By the time she had reached the last button he was back with her, sliding his hands inside to her shoulders and slipping the jumpsuit down until it fell around her feet. He kissed her again—short, quick meetings of their lips—while he unsnapped her bra, made it disappear and then sent her panties to join the rest.

Mitch kicked it all away and stepped close enough to smooth her hands up his pectorals and over his shoulders. She pulled herself against him, and slow, tingling sparks erupted as her bare skin met his inch by inch. He must have felt it, too, because he groaned softly, deep in his throat. Then he clamped his arms around her waist and fell backward onto that huge bed of his, with her on top, the long ridge of his hardness pressing against her stomach telling her that he wanted her as much as she wanted him.

He rolled with her until she was on her back and he was above her, his thigh riding the juncture of her legs. With a last flick of his tongue he abandoned her mouth to kiss her chin, to gently nibble his way along her jawline to her earlobe and then down the side of her neck to her shoulder.

"Marry me, Mitch," he half asked, half told her.

Anything, anything, she thought, just don't stop what you're doing. And indeed, anything seemed possible.

He followed the crest of her collarbone with the tip of his tongue and then dropped to take her breast into his mouth. Mitch's back arched in response, thrusting her sensitive nipple higher for his teasing, tormenting tongue. He answered by circling around and around the aureole for agonizing seconds before flicking the hardened crest.

"Say you'll marry me, Mitch," he said in a voice hoarse with passion. Then he drew her flesh deeply into his mouth.

"Oh, yes," she moaned, not sure herself whether it was in answer to his words or actions.

Need urged her to a frenzied pace. She ran her flattened palms up his back and around his shoulders to
find his two knotted male nibs. Gently pinching, rolling them between her fingers, tugging, she mimicked
what he was doing to her. But his response was nothing
akin to what hers was and so she teased him with a
feathery brush of her thumbs along his abdomen.

His reaction to that was a quick, sharp intake of
breath that made Mitch smile with satisfaction. She
didn't need to be the only one driven wild. Then the
nudge of his hips told her he wanted more and she delighted in taking a lazy course down the hair-roughened
tautness of his thighs and back up the softer inner side
before she obliged him by taking the long, hardness of
him in both hands.

The madness of desire turned him just a little rough,
not hurtful in any way, but forceful. Urgently, hungrily he tormented her breast with his mouth while his
hand traveled lower and found that spot between her
thighs that was crying out for his touch. She opened her
legs to accommodate his hand and his mouth found her
as well. Mitch gasped then, in surprise and pleasure. His
kissing, flicking and probing made desire grow and
grow until she felt as if she might explode from wanting him. She needed him fully inside her to take her to
the highest peak of what he had begun so intensely.

"Now, Patrick, now," she barely managed to whisper, in agony and ecstasy at once.

His great, magnificent body rose over her and then
joined with her, settling deep inside. Mitch wrapped her
legs around his and thrust her hips upward to meet him,
to tell him she couldn't wait anymore.

It seemed that neither could he. From the moment of
his first thrust he embedded himself completely within

her, withdrawing only to come back in again in a fast, steady, pounding rhythm. He moved with all the force Mitch needed to race up that last distance and burst into ecstasy more strongly than anytime before. At the same instant he found the peak too, and together they rode it through. Mitch felt as if he was melded into her body, into her soul, more completely than it was possible for him to be.

Slowly the wave ebbed. Little by little muscles loosened and let go. Tension and tautness eased and relaxed.

"I love you," Mitch said, feeling it deeply.

"Oh, Mitch," he sighed. "This was meant to be. Everything will be all right. I'll make sure of it."

But there was no more she could say. Every ounce of energy was spent. Patrick rolled with her yet again so that they faced each other on their sides. He smoothed her hair. He kissed her eyes. "I'll make sure of it," he whispered once more.

Before she fell asleep Mitch vaguely wondered how he meant to do that.

## Chapter Eleven

You're sure Patrick didn't say what he wanted to talk about?'' Hilly asked Mitch as the two women and Alfred went from his house into the neighboring yard.

"He only said to get you over here because the four of us needed to have a meeting. He's been on the phone in his office ever since," Mitch answered as she led the way to the picnic table where iced tea and glasses waited.

Patrick had already been out of bed when she woke up and although he had come back for a few teasing kisses that made Mitch crave more, she couldn't persuade him to delay whatever it was he was so intent on this morning.

"I assume it has something to do with the kidnapping situation," Mitch went on. "But I don't know what he's up to."

Hilly adjusted the oversize umbrella before she plopped down into one of the chairs around the glass table and stretched her spindly legs out onto Alfred's lap. "Did you kiss and make up last night?"

Mitch smiled. "I think you could say that."

"Who gave in?" Hilly asked.

"He decided to believe our story."

Just then Patrick burst out of the French doors. "Good, you're all here," he said as he joined them.

"But not for long," Alfred put in. "I have an appointment for a vitamin shot shortly." The older man cast a look at his bride and the two of them chuckled.

"That's all right because I don't think we have any time to waste. Did either of you ladies invite friends to the wedding Saturday?" Patrick asked.

Mitch looked at Hilly and Hilly at Mitch, both of them shaking their heads. It was Mitch who answered. "Alfred has taken up most of Hilly's time since we got to Colorado. We haven't made any friends close enough to invite."

He glanced at the older man. "There was a guy in a gray suit, brown shoes, balding, wore thick glasses. Did you invite him, Al?"

Alfred frowned and thought about it. "Now that you mention it I remember seeing him. I didn't know who he was. Figured he must have come as someone's date."

"Or he could be the investigator who's looking for Mitch and Hilly."

That made Mitch sit up straighter. "What makes you think so?"

Patrick recounted what Les had told him, adding how easy it would have been for a stranger to have gotten in and mingled with the guests. "And there is still an investigator hired by Hilly's son working on the case. I know that for a fact."

"How did you find that out?" Mitch asked a little tightly, seeing some of the color leave Hilly's face.

Patrick put both of his hands up, palms out. "Don't get mad. I had my detective go on looking into things in Minnesota so I'd know how I could help you. Until this morning the only thing I had heard from him was that you were wanted." His eyes held hers and his tone turned suddenly more intimate. "Everything last night came from love and belief in you, Mitch, not because I'd had your story verified already. In fact, if I still doubted you what the investigator told Les this morning wouldn't have helped."

The summer air was warm and still, but Mitch felt a shiver run up her spine. "What did he say?"

"That everything points to you having kidnapped Hilly."

"George always was thorough," Hilly said very quietly.

Mitch reached over and covered the older woman's hand with her own. Hilly's answering smile was obviously forced.

Looking back at Patrick, Mitch asked, "Why are we all here?"

"I want to do this as the launch article for *Probe*," Patrick told them without mincing words.

"No," Mitch said instantly as a surge of adrenaline shot through her.

"Hear me out, Mitch." Patrick sat forward, leaning his arms on the tabletop. "I started *Probe* for just this reason—to see that justice overrides power. What is this if not one hell of an injustice to both you and Hilly?"

It was Hilly who spoke before Mitch could. "What did you have in mind, Patrick?" she asked in that same quiet voice that suddenly sounded old and fragile to Mitch.

"We have to face facts," Patrick said to Hilly, his tone gentle but reasonable. "However trumped up and misrepresented, your son has a case against you both, Hilly. The first thing we have to do—after getting the two of you out of here and hidden somewhere safe so the investigator can't find you right away—is to get some professional support. That means for you especially, but Mitch would also need to undergo some extensive psychiatric testing. Enough so that we would have qualified experts asserting that even though you might be a little out of the mainstream you're not insane nor incompetent, and that Mitch is not some nefarious criminal who kidnapped and brainwashed you."

"No," Mitch said again, looking pointedly at Patrick and hoping her eyes relayed how strongly she was against this.

"Let him talk, Mitchy," Hilly said, prompting Patrick to go on.

"I won't kid either of you, it's going to be a fight. Anyone who would go to the lengths your son has isn't likely to concede easily. And certainly not when he has so much to lose. As you said, Mitch, the fact that the two of you have lived the way you have since you left is going to lend some credence to the theory that you're both irrational. But I think that through *Probe* we can engender public support for you as the underdogs and George as the greedy villain. With psychiatric substantiation on top of it, I'm betting that we have a chance."

"No," Mitch said yet again, more firmly than the previous times.

"It does sound a little risky, Pat," Alfred put in.

"I'm not much of a defense for Mitchy," Hilly added skeptically.

"You are if we establish that you're as sane as anyone else. And once we've documented that for over three years now she's worked odd jobs to support you both and taken good care of you, I can't see how anyone will believe she's a kidnapper."

"The whole thing is out of the question, Patrick," Mitch said heatedly, wondering if he had paid any attention at all to what she'd told him about the two months she and Hilly had spent in her cabin.

But again Hilly spoke up before Mitch's objection was addressed. "I don't know, Patrick. My son is a well-respected man with more power under his belt by now. And as much as he wants the money he has a vengeance against Mitch. I'm afraid that even if I pass a psychiatric evaluation, it won't be enough to keep her from being tried."

"The two of you have lived with the fear of this for a long time now. I understand how that gains strength for George and makes you think your case is weaker. But I wouldn't even suggest putting you through it if I didn't believe you could win. Think about what it would mean to both of you. To all of us. You wouldn't have to spend every minute watching over your shoulder for who might be suspicious or following you. No more moving around and living a fugitive life-style. *Probe* can expose George, exonerate Mitch and reinstate you, Hilly, as the head of the fortune that's rightfully yours."

"I don't care about the money," Hilly said distractedly, frowning into the distance for a moment. Then, as if she were thinking aloud, she said, "What would it mean to George?"

"You have to consider yourself and Mitch," Patrick urged.

But Hilly didn't seem to hear. Instead she continued talking to herself. "The least would be humiliation, his reputation—maybe his whole life—destroyed. The worst might be jail for pretending it was a kidnapping when he knew full well it wasn't, and pulling the FBI in on it for all these years."

Mitch squeezed the elderly woman's hand and shot daggers at Patrick with her eyes.

"Hilly," he said gently.

But again she didn't respond.

"Hilly?" Mitch called to her.

It took several moments before the older woman jerked slightly and looked at Mitch as if no one else was with them.

"Are you all right?" Mitch asked.

Hilly didn't answer readily. But after a while she nodded. "Yes."

"Hilly." Patrick finally managed to gain her attention. "I know he's your son no matter what. But he's done a terrible thing to you and to Mitch. He's done something that has to be righted or it could ruin Mitch's entire life."

"If you truly care for me, Patrick," Mitch cut in in a tone that was at once strong, protective and warning, "you'll drop this now."

He looked at her, his brow furrowed, and shook his head. "It's because I love you that I can't. If you don't get free of the unfinished business in your past you...we won't have any future."

"I don't want a future at this expense," she said sternly.

Hilly broke the deadlock of Mitch and Patrick's eyes when she inhaled audibly. Then, drawing herself up, she glanced at Mitch. Her smile was sad but genuine. "It's up to you, Mitchy. I've lost about all I can lose. If you're willing to take the chance of having me be your defense in order to have a life with Patrick then I'm willing to give it my best shot."

Mitch shook her head vehemently.

Hilly waved away the denial. "Think it over. You've done enough for me and whatever happens to George he brought on with his own actions. It's time to consider yourself and the rest of your life." She slipped her hand out from under Mitch's and smoothed Mitch's cheek lovingly. Then she pushed herself up from her chair as wearily as her age might dictate and reached for Alfred's arm. "We'd better leave these two to talk and get you to your appointment."

Alfred stood but he narrowed his eyes on Patrick. "I'm trusting you to do right by my girl here," he warned.

"I wouldn't do anything else," Patrick answered, but he was looking at Mitch when he said it.

Mitch watched the older couple leave, waiting until she heard Alfred's sliding glass door open and close so she knew Hilly was out of earshot. Then she turned to Patrick. "The answer is no."

"You've been saying that since I started this. I don't think you've heard a word I've said."

"Funny, I wondered if you had heard what I said when I told you about what this had all done to Hilly before."

"I didn't miss a word. I also don't think those two months when she was out of her head are so likely to reoccur that this shouldn't be pursued."

"And I think that there isn't anything worth putting it to the test."

"She's protecting you and you're protecting her, and neither one of you is coming out ahead, Mitch."

"I won't sacrifice Hilly for my own sake. She's not young. She married Alfred so she could settle down and have peace. The last thing she needs is to have this turned into a public spectacle, especially when her son has enough evidence of her zaniness to put her away if she loses."

"This isn't a fight you'll lose."

"You don't know that. And even if it was a guaranteed win, you saw what bringing it all up again did to her. The subject is so powerful that was all it took to make her mind wander, to take her out of herself." Mitch sat forward in her chair, her posture a plea for him to see her side.

"Having her own son turn against her the way he did left deeper scars than the marks he made on her skin. Do you think she wants the whole world to know about it? Do you think she wants to announce what kind of a person he is? You're talking about publicly humiliating her. I told you before that I would never say anything against George in front of her. When she first came out of those two months in the cabin she said that in some way she must have been responsible for what he did because she was, after all, his mother, that she had raised him. After that she never said a word against him. You saw for yourself that she still thinks of protecting him."

Patrick reached over and took her hand, smoothing the back of it with his thumb in a soothing gesture. "I didn't say it would be easy on her, or easy on you, either, for that matter. But Al and I will be there for you in any way you need us."

"Don't you see that to bring this out in the open would rob her of her dignity? You could be exposing her to ridicule and condemnation as the lunatic George claims she is. At seventy-eight she shouldn't have to be put under a public microscope. And certainly never on my account."

"It would clear her name, too, Mitch. Don't forget that. And recoup a fortune that's rightfully hers."

"Do you really think either of those is worth what this could do to her? Because I don't." Mitch pulled her hand out from under his and sat back in her chair.

"And do you really think the two of you can go on forever eluding private investigators and the FBI? Be realistic. It's incredible that you've done it this long. You're going to have to face it sooner or later. Hell, for all we know it could already be later. The two Peeping Tom incidents and the strange man at the wedding could mean everything is closing in on you right now." He took a breath and seemed to consciously change his tone from reproaching back to reasoning. "Everything you've said about the weak points in your cases is true. What you need is the kind of public support *Probe* can get you. Now is the time, Mitch."

"For which of us, Patrick? Hilly and me, or you and your magazine? Maybe you're just using our situation for your own purposes. After all, you've been looking for something with just enough scandal and human interest. There's plenty of scandal in this one and a nutty old lady is always good for the human interest part. That makes us perfect, doesn't it?"

"You know better than that."

"Do I? Maybe that's why you had one of your magazine's investigators look into my background. Why not kill two birds with one stone? Find out what you had no business knowing unless I chose to tell you, and get a launch article for your magazine out of it to boot."

For a moment he stared at her, his expression harsh. When he spoke again his voice was low. "Do you really think I'm the kind of person who would do something like that?"

"I'm beginning to wonder," she shot at him angrily.

"It's for your sake," he said through clenched teeth. "I can find other stories for *Probe*"

"Good, then do it."

"And leave this hanging over your head like an ax when I know—I *know*, dammit—that when the public gets wind of this you'll have the force of a mass of people backing you up? Not to do it would be crazier than anything you've done so far."

"You can't *know* that anyone would support us. Look at yourself as the test case, Patrick, because you were the first person I ever told. You didn't believe me. How can I hope anyone else will? My story was farfetched, isn't that what you called it? And yet you think strangers are going to not only believe it but come out with some kind of mass appeal for Hilly and me to be vindicated? I think *that's* farfetched."

"Dammit, Mitch, I told you my doubts came out of my own hang-up. I had too much history clouding my thoughts. But that wouldn't come into play with the public."

"You forget that I've already had trial by media once before and lost."

"You don't know that you lost."

"I know what I read. Every time I picked up another paper I was guiltier than the time before. With all of George's connections I'm sure he had it slanted the way he wanted, and no matter what *Probe* prints, those old stories are bound to resurface. I think you're naive to believe public support would be all that great."

"*Probe* will document everything. We'll go all the way back to your parents dying and Hilly taking you in. We'll interview everybody who's ever known either of you. We'll do a psychological profile on her son, track you through every city you've been in since you left, do in-depth profiles on the two of you. Your side will get more exposure and, therefore, more of a hearing than it could in any other way, refuting everything that came before. That's the whole purpose of *Probe*."

"And in the process you get a dynamo of a launch. Let's not forget that."

"You can't get away from that, can you? Yes, it would be a great launch. Yes, it's exactly what I've been looking for. Is that what you want to hear? But it doesn't have a damn thing to do with this. Why can't you see that?"

"Because I care about Hilly and what I *can* see is how much harm it could do to her."

"Well, I care about you. I love you. What kind of future are we going to have if we don't do this? Are you going to marry me and disappear two months later because somebody looks cross-eyed at you in the grocery store? And when will that be? Tomorrow? The next day? You can't go on the way you have. No matter how much you wish it wasn't so, Hilly's at the end of her life. What happens to you when she dies? How many more decades are you going to be on the run? Or in jail because she isn't around to defend you at all? Wake up, for crying out loud. It's over. It's time to face it and fight."

"No," she said yet again, her voice soft. "Not at Hilly's expense."

Silence fell then, palpable with tension. Mitch met his glorious blue eyes squarely to let him know she wouldn't back down.

Patrick shook his head and sighed. "Then maybe I'll just have to do it without your consent."

Everything was so still Mitch could hear her pounding heartbeat. "You wouldn't do that."

"Better that than to see you go on running."

"I don't believe you would be selfish enough to launch your magazine with Hilly's blood."

"I have a selfish motive, all right. But it isn't *Probe*. It's personal. I love you, Mitch, and I want you. I want us to have the rest of our lives together, I want us to end up like Hilly and Alfred are starting out. But we can't do that with this shadowing us. I know this is what needs to be done. For my sake, for yours, for Hilly's, for our future together and for Hilly and Al's. Hilly has already half agreed. I can persuade her the rest of the way because it's what's best for you and even if she doesn't know it now, I can make her see it. I can keep the detective digging and put the rest of *Probe*'s people on it full speed. And I can clear you with or without your cooperation."

"It would have to be without," she said very softly. "Without my cooperation and without me."

"Do it and I lose you for sure, is that it?" he asked just as quietly.

"Yes." She didn't hesitate even though its meaning choked her. "If your only motives are personal you'd defeat your own purpose."

For the second time their eyes met and locked, and tension-filled silence returned. Mitch could see Patrick's struggle in his expression and inside she pleaded with him not to do it. His brow creased and his features tightened visibly.

"I love you. I want you," he said again, even more decisively. "But if I have to lose you to save you from going on the way you have and ultimately being caught when it's too late..." He paused. "Then I'll do it."

Mitch felt as if she were drowning. "Please don't," she asked in a near whisper. "You don't understand what you're doing to Hilly."

"She's tougher than you think."

Mitch just shook her head in denial.

"Then fight it with her," he entreated. "Give her your strength."

Again Mitch shook her head. "I'll take her away if I can persuade her to go with me. If I can't..." The thought of what she was saying made her voice crack. She cleared her throat and finished with as much determination as she could muster. "If I can't I won't stay to watch you hurt her."

"Mitch," he said loudly. "Dammit, I won't hurt either of you. Trust me."

She wanted to. She loved him. There was nothing she wanted more than him, his love, to be a part of his life. But vivid in her mind was the memory of Hilly during those two months—fearful, demented, devitalized, enfeebled—and nothing could make Mitch agree to risk that happening to her again.

She felt her chin quiver. Her eyes stung. "Not even for you," she whispered in answer to her own thoughts.

"I'm going to do it anyway, Mitch," he told her flatly, sadly. "For you and for Hilly."

Once more Mitch shook her head. She stood and for a moment stared at him. Then, forcing vigor she didn't feel into her voice, she said, "Goodbye, Patrick," and turned away.

"Mitch," he called to her back as she left him.

But she didn't stop. She had given up everything for Hilly's sake once before, she could do it again.

Even when it meant giving up Patrick.

## Chapter Twelve

Mitch expected the house to be empty when she stormed in. She jammed the sliding door closed so hard the glass quivered. Then she made a sharp left turn and pounded her fists on the kitchen counter before dropping her head down on them with a barely muffled shriek.

But adrenaline was pumping all through her and she couldn't stay that way for long. With an agonized sigh she stood back up one vertebra at a time until she was straight.

Damn him, damn him, damn him.

Why did he have to make this all so much worse than it was? Why couldn't he be like Alfred? Why couldn't he just accept things the way they were and go on as if the whole situation was in the past?

But not Patrick. He was going to charge in and right the wrong. Whether she wanted him to or not. Damn him.

She had to think what to do and began to pace. In front of the breakfast nook. Around the kitchen. Down the hall into the foyer. As she did an about-face at the front door for the return trip she caught sight of something in the living room and stopped short. Hilly was sitting on the sofa.

The energy drained out of Mitch instantly. She watched the older woman, keeping as still as Hilly. So motionless was she that Mitch's first thought was that she'd had a heart attack or a stroke. But then she saw the elderly woman blink, and knew better, even though it offered only marginal relief. Hilly was so quiet, so lost inside herself that she hadn't heard Mitch's door-slamming or pacing, or noticed Mitch as she stood in the entrance watching her. The only other time Mitch had ever seen Hilly like this was during those two months after George's beating.

A shiver went up Mitch's spine and her determination not to have Patrick bring everything up again calcified. She stepped into the living room. "Hilly?"

Hilly didn't budge, didn't even seem to hear.

It's happening again, Mitch thought. "Hilly? Are you all right?" she said louder.

Hilly's head jolted up. Her eyebrows arched and she blinked rapidly, as if just waking up. Then she frowned and looked confused. She turned her face toward Mitch, asking foggily, "Did you say something?"

"I asked if you're all right."

Hilly thought about it for a moment before answering. Or maybe her mind wandered somewhere else—Mitch couldn't tell. But finally she said, "Yes. Fine."

Mitch went to sit beside Hilly, positioning herself so she could watch her as she talked. "I thought you were going with Alfred for his vitamin shot?"

Again it took Hilly a while to assimilate the question. "Oh, I was. But since he said he didn't mind going alone I decided to stay home."

"I see." Mitch nodded, all the while studying the older woman. The usually rosy-red color in her cheeks was gone and her face seemed drawn, old. "I want us both to leave, Hil," Mitch said straight out.

Hilly inhaled so deeply that her shoulders lifted. They dropped back when she sighed. "I knew that's what you were going to say."

"Because that's what we have to do," Mitch insisted gently.

"Do we?" Hilly answered, sounding confused and whimsical.

"You know it's likely that the stranger at the wedding was George's investigator." Mitch paused to gauge Hilly's response. There wasn't any. She went on anyway. "Patrick is intent on using us to launch his magazine, even though I told him not to. He thinks he can talk you into it and so long as he has your cooperation he doesn't care that I'm against it."

Hilly's frown deepened, drawing her fluffy white eyebrows together. She looked at Mitch. "That doesn't sound like Patrick."

"He's convinced the article and public support are the only way to get us out of this."

"Maybe he's right." The older woman's gaze strayed again.

"We've done okay on our own."

Hilly shook her head. "I meant it when I said I promised Alfred that I'd stay."

"He could come with us," Mitch said anxiously. "Or you could arrange some way to get letters to him and he could visit wherever we are. Maybe when things die down here we could come back."

Hilly looked at her again. "I believe we can trust Patrick."

"Can we? Remember that regardless of what happens to us he gets himself just what he needs to launch his magazine."

"Mitchy," Hilly chastised, but she sounded so much more like her usual self that Mitch was glad to hear it. "You can't think he's just out for himself in this."

"It won't do him any harm. But it could do us a lot of it."

"He wouldn't let that happen," the older woman argued with a little of her spunk returned.

"He couldn't stop it."

"I think he'd find a way. He loves you. He wouldn't let you go to jail."

"Even people who are loved go to jail, Hil. There's nothing he could do to change it if George's accusations stood up in court. Then we'd both be in the soup."

"Couldn't we let him write it and just see what happens? If things are going against us we could run away then."

"By then our faces would have been splashed all over a national magazine and there wouldn't be a place we could go without being recognized. Remember how much worse it was when that was true before? We had to wear disguises and make sure we weren't seen together and I had to work as a telephone solicitor rather than chance working out in the open."

"I don't believe you want to leave Patrick," Hilly said contrarily.

"There isn't a choice." Mitch's voice cracked.

"You don't know how much I want to stay here and live a normal life, Mitchy."

The trouble was Mitch did know, because she wanted it as much as Hilly did. "There is one alternative," she said hesitantly, loathing the thought.

"What's that?"

"It isn't foolproof. It's risky." And it made a cold lump form in the pit of Mitch's stomach. But she didn't say that. "I could leave alone to decoy whoever has traced us here. That way you could stay. If you absolutely refuse to cooperate with Patrick's story, he might not go through with it and the whole thing could end for you."

"But not for you."

Mitch took a deep breath and thought of a way to convince Hilly. "Actually it might," she said as if it were a preferable plan. "It would be easier for me alone to blend into the crowd and with the investigator still looking for two women I could eventually lose him."

"But Mitchy, you'd be all by yourself."

Mitch shrugged as if that didn't matter. "Not for long. Once I settle down I'd meet new people and have a normal life, too."

"But without Patrick."

Again she shrugged. "There'd be another Patrick," she lied.

"You don't mean that."

"It's a way for us to have regular lives, Hil."

For a time neither of them said anything, only now it was Mitch whose eyes wandered as Hilly scrutinized her, the older woman obviously back to her old keenly aware self. Then Hilly broke the silence.

"You love Patrick," she said as if she had read it in Mitchy's face. "That doesn't happen for real many times in a life. Don't think of me, Mitchy. Think of yourself and Patrick." Hilly paused, reached over and squeezed Mitch's hand. "But I'll leave it up to you. If you won't stay and let the article be done, then we'll both go."

Through the picture window just then they could see Alfred pulling into the driveway. Hilly patted Mitch's hand reassuringly and stood. "I think I'm going to catch him and make him take me for a ride so you can have some time alone to think. Just keep in mind that I'm game to letting it all hang out, Mitchy. I think we could beat this rap." She finished with a thumbs-up sign and a semblance of her old vigor.

Mitch could only smile wanly and watch as the older woman left, calling to Alfred from the front door before she closed it after herself.

The house seemed abysmally quiet when Hilly had gone. Mitch suddenly felt overwhelmingly tired. She closed her eyes and lay down, her head on the cushion Hilly had just left. "What am I going to do?" she moaned. Then a second later she answered herself as if it were a solution, "Go take a bath."

It might not resolve anything, but the warm water felt wonderful, she reasoned when she sank into the tub several minutes later. She rested her head on the marble edge and turned on the whirlpool, hungry for the hum to fill the quiet that made her thoughts ring too loudly in her mind. But even muted, they couldn't be escaped.

What would it do to the older woman to take her away from Alfred and this place where she wanted to stay? Nothing good, seemed to be the answer to that.

More and more Mitch was aware of Hilly's age and increasing fragility. Not that Hilly was exactly frail—she could still keep up with Jack LaLanne and not get winded. But she wasn't as resilient as she'd been a year or two ago, either. Then, Hilly would never have admitted to needing a rest or to not having the energy to move again. That wasn't the truth now.

Realizing that ruled out the two of them leaving. For the first time Mitch admitted it to herself and actually accepted it. She knew that Hilly would go with her if she chose to run again. But she also knew that Hilly wouldn't last much longer living nomadically. That it would wear her down and Mitch would end up losing her anyway.

Mitch sank below the surface of the water and held her breath until her lungs burned. The physical pain was preferable to the wrenching of her heart at the idea of losing Hilly—an old childhood fear.

But Mitch wasn't a child anymore. And Hilly was twenty-one years closer to the end of her life.

If leaving without Hilly was the only chance to spare the older woman any more of having to be on the run or having the ugliness of the past exposed, then she was going to have to choose losing Hilly in the way that was best for Hilly.

Mitch came up for air. Now it was her eyes that stung. She would have to leave when Hilly didn't realize that's what she was doing. And she'd have to write the older woman a letter telling her not to allow Patrick to do the article. Once she was gone she knew Hilly would do anything to protect her, and she felt reasonably sure the elderly woman wouldn't chance letting Patrick go through with it against Mitch's wishes.

She slid underwater again. *Burn lungs, burn. Better that than my heart ripping apart.* Because thoughts of Patrick reminded her that she would be leaving him behind, too, and that was what it made her feel. Damn it all.

What kind of an alternative was it to have to leave the only two people in the world she loved? A rotten one.

This time she stayed underwater until her head grew light, but neither burning lungs nor light-headedness canceled out the slicing pain in her heart. She gave in and pushed herself to sit up. With her elbows on her thighs she dropped her face into her hands.

Could she really leave behind both Patrick and Hilly? She had to.

A wetness much warmer than the bathwater rolled into her palms. Dammit, dammit, dammit it all. But what other choice did she have? To stay and let Patrick publish the whole ugly, sordid mess? And yet that was the single answer to not losing both Patrick and Hilly.

How would Patrick handle the article? she wondered suddenly. It hadn't occurred to her to ask. Was there a way it could be done and preserve Hilly's dignity? That, with the support of Mitch and Alfred and Patrick, wouldn't take such a toll on the older woman.

It didn't seem possible, she had to admit. And yet what would it do to Hilly to have Mitch just disappear on her? How much of a toll would that take?

It wouldn't be easy on her, Mitch knew that. It wouldn't be any easier for Hilly to lose Mitch than for Mitch to lose Hilly. The older woman wasn't a worrier, but when she did it she could make herself sick with it.

*Oh, Patrick, can I trust you to find a way to serve us up on a platter without skewering us in the process?*

What did she think? a little voice in her head asked. That Patrick was some kind of tabloid journalist? That he would sensationalize their story? That didn't seem like Patrick. But what did seem like Patrick then? If she thought he would use this situation for his own purposes, why didn't she think he'd do it with yellow journalism?

That made her stop and reconsider.

She honestly did not believe Patrick would handle this with any sensationalism. So did she really think he was the kind of person who would expose them for his own purposes? She didn't.

Now, when she wasn't in the fresh throes of fear and anger and outrage, she knew that deep down she didn't believe he was that sort of man. She couldn't picture him exploiting anyone. After all, wasn't he starting *Probe* in the first place to right that kind of injustice? Exploitation would be a contradiction to what had become the goal of his career. He had too much integrity, too much sympathy and sensitivity, too much honesty to do what she had accused.

Mitch took her hands away from her face and straightened. Yes, she could trust Patrick to do this in a way that would only help both her and Hilly, she realized. Because on top of everything else, she knew he loved her too much to do anything that would hurt her. She also knew, with a sudden clarity, that leaving Patrick behind, for any reason, was something she would regret forever.

But just when she was beginning to feel that there might be hope she reminded herself that no matter what kind of person Patrick was, it didn't change what exposure might do to Hilly. The slight buoyancy of

Mitch's spirits deflated. No matter how she looked at it, it seemed she was going to lose Patrick.

But if there was a different perspective with which to see Patrick, maybe there was a different perspective with which to see Hilly's side in all of this. If she were Hilly, she thought, would it be more harmful to have Mitch leave without a word, or face the fight with George?

A hard choice—between Mitch or her own son. But her son had abused her. Her son meant to steal from her, to have her institutionalized. Mitch didn't know if she was seeing herself as more important to Hilly than Hilly might, but there seemed to be more reason for the older woman to opt for Mitch rather than for George.

Being a decoy was no guarantee that one or both of them wouldn't be found anyway. It was only a guarantee that if it happened they wouldn't be together to face it. Mitch knew that she could stand up to George's charges and fight much better with the support and love of Hilly and Alfred and Patrick. If that was true for her, then maybe it was true for Hilly, too, the way Patrick had insisted.

Was she just talking herself into all of this because she wanted Patrick so much? She did want him. She loved him, she wanted to spend the rest of her life with him. It felt more right than anything she could ever remember. But the more she thought about Hilly, the more cruel it seemed to disappear without a trace and leave her to worry and possibly face being found without Mitch by her side.

No, she hadn't talked herself into it because she loved Patrick. He wasn't the whole reason. Having a life with him was just the up side of a hard choice.

Mitch turned off the whirlpool. Into the sudden silence came two sharp rings of the doorbell as if the ringer was impatient. It was Patrick, was Mitch's first thought. He had come to convince her of what she had already decided and since she wouldn't have heard his knocks on the back door he had gone around to the front to ring the bell.

She lunged up out of the tub and grabbed the first thing she could lay her hands on—Alfred's terry-cloth robe. Dripping wet, she shrugged into it and tied the sash around her waist as she ran out of the bathroom and down the stairs.

Everything will be all right. Patrick will make sure everything is all right, she chanted to herself on the way.

The sound of two male voices talking in front of the door stopped her from flinging it open. It didn't seem likely that Patrick would have brought someone with him. So as not to be seen, in case it wasn't Patrick, Mitch carefully moved aside the panel curtain on the pencil-thin window beside the door and peeked out.

It wasn't Patrick at all. Instead three men dressed in poorly tailored suits stood there, talking very seriously to a fourth man in a police uniform. Mitch's heart nearly stopped.

Because most of the people at Hilly and Alfred's wedding were strangers to her, the man who had been asking questions then hadn't meant anything to her. But now she recognized one of the three men in suits as someone she had seen that day. From there it wasn't a big step to realize that the man was indeed George's investigator and had called in the authorities.

She tiptoed into the den. The four shutters on the window there were closed. Stealthily she went to them and very carefully eased one of the slats so she could see out. Parked at the curb were two police cars with three more officers standing outside of them. In the driveway was a plain white sedan with federal government license plates—confirmation that the jig was up.

For a moment Mitch froze. She couldn't think of what to do and for some reason she had the sense that up until that moment this had all been a game she hadn't taken seriously enough. But George's detective, the police officers and the other three men who she could only guess to be FBI agents, were all too real. And she doubted if they would feel inclined to politely sip tea while she told them her story.

Just then she heard someone from the front porch call to the policemen at the curb to see if they could find a way around back. Mitch knew if she was going to get out of this the back door and the hedge gate to Patrick's were her only hope.

She dashed out of the den, across the foyer and down the hallway as the doorbell rang again, even more insistently than before. In the kitchen she slowed down enough to glance out the window over the sink to be sure no one had made it into the backyard yet.

When the sliding glass door stuck she rued having slammed it. "Open, open," she whispered as she pulled on the handle. All at once it did, costing her her balance for a moment before she charged out.

She ran around the pool and made a beeline for the hedge gate. As she reached it she heard voices just beyond the front fence. Willing the gate not to squeak she opened it just wide enough to slip through, then pulled it closed after herself. She had barely made it to the tiles that surrounded Patrick's pool when she heard Alfred's front gate open. She ran as fast as she could toward the French doors. They were locked.

Mitch couldn't believe it. Patrick rarely locked them unless he was gone. It was the first time it occurred to her that he might not still be home. She forced herself to take a deep breath and try again. Maybe they were just stuck.

No luck. The doors were locked tight.

How long would it take for the police to try the hedge gate or start searching the neighborhood and find her huddling in Patrick's backyard wearing only Alfred's robe?

The sound of a male voice from the other yard put her back into action. She tried the doors yet again. Don't be gone, Patrick, she silently lamented. I need you.

As if in answer she suddenly realized she could hear the shower running in the bathroom off his bedroom. At the same time orders came from Alfred's backyard for someone to check the grounds and see where that gate led to. Without another thought Mitch hiked up the robe, stepped onto one of the lawn chairs and climbed onto the glass tabletop so she could reach the bathroom window.

"Patrick?" she whispered through the screen so no one next door would hear her. But Patrick didn't hear her, either.

At that height she could see part of Alfred's yard. A uniformed policeman was going up to the house while another headed in the direction of the hedge. Her heart was beating a mile a minute. She had to get through that screen into the house. Mitch pushed on it with both of her hands. It bowed but didn't break.

"Patrick?" she tried a second time. Again there was no response.

She didn't know what else to do, so she braced both of her hands on the window ledge and, using her head like a battering ram, she butted the screen out of its frame.

With a last furtive glance over the hedge to make sure no one was looking in her direction she hoisted herself onto the ledge and swung first one leg then the other inside. With her heels on the towel bar below, she was about to lower herself to the floor when the shower stopped and Patrick pushed back the curtain.

"What the hell is this?" he demanded harshly, his expression showing no pleasure at all.

Mitch swallowed. She tried to smile but could feel that it was a weak imitation. "I really was going to come in through one of the doors and do this right, but . . ." She glanced out the window at the sound of the hedge gate being opened, and jumped down quickly. "I'm afraid I'm about to be arrested."

## Chapter Thirteen

So you're about to be arrested,'' Patrick said caustically as he yanked down a towel that was draped over the shower rod, and dried his chest. ''Cut your escape short, did it?''

Somehow she hadn't expected him to be mad at her. ''I wasn't going to escape,'' she told him hurriedly. ''In fact I had decided to stay and take you up on the article and the help in fighting George and—'' She could hardly say *take you up on your marriage proposal* when his reaction was less than welcoming, so she cut herself off.

Patrick only frowned down at her.

''This is no time to doubt me, Patrick,'' she said.

He watched her for a moment more while he finished toweling off. Then he sighed. She had the impression that he was going to leave that discussion for later and deal with her more imminent problems now.

"What's going on?" he asked as he crossed in front of her and left the bathroom.

Mitch followed, only peripherally aware of both his nakedness and how ludicrous this situation was. "I was in the tub when the doorbell rang," she began, giving him a quick account of what had led her here while he pulled on a pair of black tennis shorts and a white T-shirt. But rather than say anything when she had finished he merely turned and left the bedroom.

Mitch trailed him down the hallway and into the living room, ducking quickly back into the hall when she realized the drapes were open on the side window that allowed a partial view of Alfred's front yard.

"Well, you've drawn a crowd," he observed sardonically as he came back to stand in front of her. "There are five police cars, two unmarked sedans, most of Maplewood Estates' residents and security. You really are a desperate criminal, aren't you?"

Mitch took a breath to hold on to her patience and said, "I understand that you're angry because I walked out this morning—"

He cut her off. "And because you didn't care enough about me and spending your life with me—the way you led me to believe you did—to face up to a ridiculous situation that had unfairly condemned you. But now that you can't get out of it you want me to do something. Right?"

Mitch pushed a damp strand of hair away from her face. She was acutely aware that she was not at her best and that this was no time to have to convince him that she really did love him and couldn't have gone through with leaving. "If I tell you the truth you won't believe me anyway, so why don't you help me out of this mess. Then when it's over and you see that I stay with you anyway just because I love you, maybe you'll be convinced," she blurted out, spurred by fear and frustration.

"Don't lay that unreasonable doubting stuff on me this time, Mitch. I may have been guilty of it before, but not now. You threw my offer in my face, accused me of wanting to do it for my own gains and walked out. It seems to me that if you really did love me you would have done anything it took for us to have a future together. Put yourself in my shoes. How would this look to you?"

"Okay, fine," she spat out, flinging a hand in the air in one of Hilly's dramatic gestures. "Then why don't you just turn me in and watch them haul me off to jail. Will that make you feel better? Or maybe you'd rather I save you the trouble and turn myself in."

She took a step around him but his hand shot out to her arm to stop her. Mitch raised her chin and challenged him with her eyes. His were shadowed beneath an ominous frown but when he spoke his voice wasn't as harsh as his expression. "Do you mean it?"

"Do I mean what? That I love you and had decided to stay even before the game was up? That I have every intention of proving it to you if I get out of this now? Or that I'll turn myself in?" she asked angrily.

"Not that you'll turn yourself in."

"Yes, I meant the rest. But you'll have to trust me because I don't have any way to prove it at the moment."

His pale blue eyes held hers. Then without revealing anything he released her arm. "Go in and put on something of mine. I'll make some phone calls and see what I can find out."

Mitch felt a certain amount of relief just in knowing he was going to do what he could. "Thank you," she said quietly and headed back to his bedroom.

"Where are Hilly and Al?" he called after her.

"They went for a drive." She quickly pulled on a navy-blue T-shirt and a white pair of tennis shorts, cinching the drawstring to keep them up. Then she went back down the hall, joining him in the family room. "Seeing all the commotion out front ought to warn them not to come back."

Patrick punched a number on the telephone and stretched the cord to the window. Unlike in the living room, these drapes were pulled, so he poked a finger through them and peered out. "Think again. Al just drove up and parked at the end of my driveway."

A shiver ran through Mitch. "Is Hilly with him?"

"Can't tell. No, he just got out alone."

"Where's Hilly?"

Patrick only shrugged as he spoke into the phone, asking for Les.

All Mitch could do was pace as Patrick made several more calls. On each trip into the family room she spied through the curtains. Not that she saw much. Alfred had disappeared into the house with all but two of the policemen who were left outside. More and more neighbors milled around, but nowhere among them could Mitch find Hilly.

The next half hour passed with Mitch clenching and unclenching her fists, wondering where Hilly was, worrying about her, wondering who Patrick was talking to and worrying about it, wondering what was going on at Alfred's house and worrying about it.

She was turning into the kitchen to vary her pacing route when Patrick put his hand over the phone's mouthpiece and said her name. She stopped dead in her tracks and shot a hopeful glance at him.

"Don't you hear that tapping? It sounds like it's coming from my office. You'd better go see what it is."

So enmeshed was she in her wondering and worrying that Mitch hadn't heard it. But now she realized that there actually was a sound like something knocking on a window coming from the far side of the house. She ran all the way to Patrick's office. But once there she opened the door only a crack to peek inside. The drapes were pulled aside and Hilly's face was on the other side.

"Hilly!" Mitch rushed in. It took her a moment to figure out how to unlock the window.

"It's about time, Mitchy. I've been out here forever," Hilly said when the glass finally slid open.

A second wave of relief washed through Mitch as she maneuvered the screen free and helped the elderly woman climb in. "Where have you been? Alfred came home a long time ago."

"When we saw that mess outside he dropped me off a couple of blocks away so I could sneak in. But there are police all over the place. I had to duck from bush to bush to get here."

"Are you all right?"

Hilly fanned the air. "Fine. Alfred's going to do what he can to forestall things and try to get a hold of Judge Thorpe, though I don't know that there's anything he can do." The older woman took in Mitch's clothes and arched a shocked eyebrow. "What have you been up to? Alfred and I thought you were probably chained to a chair next door while they all waited for me to show up. I didn't expect to find you here."

As Mitch took Hilly into the family room she briefly explained the events that had transpired since the older woman had left her.

Patrick was just hanging up the phone when they came into the room. "Hilly. I was hoping it was you," he greeted without enthusiasm, his expression solemn. "Just in time, too. I have something to talk to you about."

"That sounds ominous," Hilly said as she sat on the couch.

Mitch sat on the corner of the coffee table directly in front of Hilly and raised her gaze expectantly to Patrick who didn't seem to relish what he was about to say.

"After a lot of machinations I finally got through to your son and his attorneys. He has a proposition for you." Patrick moved to sit on the arm of the sofa, right beside Hilly. He reached down, took the elderly woman's hand in his and patted it. "Hold on to your hat, old girl," he said in a quiet, reassuring tone that eased some of the tension in the room.

"Your son is willing to inform the authorities that after all this time you have just contacted him with the news that you left of your own volition, in the company of Mitch but not kidnapped by her, and that the entire incident was just another in a long line of your eccentric behavior. Apparently there has always been a theory that the ransom note was a crank, and this will just confirm it. Without his insistence that you're out of your mind, your word won't be suspect and you and Mitch will both be off the hook." He stopped.

Hilly urged him to go on, her voice tight, controlled and harsh. "What does he want for that?"

"He wants you to relinquish all claim to the Halvorsen estate—money, homes and all business holdings."

After another moment of silence Hilly laughed a short, mirthless burst of air. "Greedy to the end, isn't he?" she said ruefully.

"It's blackmail," Mitch named it unnecessarily, her tone relaying the contempt she felt for the man. "You don't have to agree, Hil. We could still take our chances with Patrick's magazine."

"That would take time we don't have," Hilly said reasonably. "While Patrick compiles everything and gets his magazine out on the stands you'll wait in jail and I'll end up reading the article from the sunroom of the nearest asylum." She shook her head wearily. "We can end this here and now. I think if George wants it all this badly he might as well have it."

The sadness in Hilly's voice broke Mitch's heart. "I'm sorry, Hil," was all she could manage in a cracked voice, reaching for the older woman's other hand.

But Hilly rallied faster than Mitch expected. Taking a deep breath she pulled her shoulders back and looked up at Patrick with a wry curve to her lips. "I hope you think more highly of your mother," she said. "Give him the go-ahead. He can have whatever he wants, just get him to call off his dogs and leave Mitchy and me in peace." Then she looked over at Mitch and winked. "We have better things to do, don't we?"

It was after ten that night before everything was squared away. Hilly had had to sign a preliminary agreement dictated to a local attorney and brought to Patrick's house before her son would notify the authorities. Then once word was passed on to the police and FBI, they weren't satisfied until Mitch and Hilly presented themselves at Alfred's house and answered a battery of questions. When it was all finally over Hilly slipped into Alfred's arms for a reassuring hug. Then the older couple wearily climbed the stairs to their bedroom. That left Mitch alone with Patrick.

She locked the front door and turned to find him watching her. "It's been quite a day," she said, for lack of anything better with which to break the silence.

He didn't say anything but took her hand and pulled her behind him through the house, back door and hedge gate.

The trip did wonders for Mitch's overstrung nerves.

The day had been too hectic and harried for them to have exchanged anything but necessary conversation. It had left her unsure of what was going to be between her and Patrick when it was all over with. But taking her back to his house didn't seem like the act of a man who had washed his hands of her. Until he swept her up into his arms and dumped her in his swimming pool.

Mitch came up sputtering water. "What was that for?" she demanded as she smoothed her hair back out of her eyes.

"For not trusting me to get you cleared or to be careful of Hilly's feelings, for accusing me of selfish motives and for walking out on me this morning."

She splashed water his way but he jumped back in time to miss the drenching. "Okay, so it took me a little while to think it over. Is that a crime?"

"Not if you had said 'let me think about it.' It is when you did what you did and stabbed me through the heart in the process."

"I'm sorry," she said with a shiver. Then she raised her hand. "Help me out?"

Patrick took her hand but when Mitch tried to pull him in with her he only smiled smugly and hoisted her up. "Very funny, Cuddy," he said of her attempt to even the score. "Or is that really your name?"

Mitch pulled the wet shirt away from her skin, wringing out the hem. "Michelle Marie Cuddington, at your service."

"Michelle Marie Cuddington," he repeated as if feeling the words. "That sounds very upper crust. You wouldn't be keeping more secrets from me, would you?"

"I was born in Minneapolis to Marie and Martin Cuddington thirty-three years ago. My mother was an art collector, my father invented a cog that revolutionized engine exhaust systems from which royalties and residuals are still gathering in several accounts in Minnesota banks—unless I'm mistaken since I haven't been able to keep up with it or use any of the money for the past few years."

"Michelle Marie Cuddington, how much money are we talking about here?"

"Careful Drake, or I could take you for a gold digger."

"How much?"

She squeezed water out of her sleeves. "I don't know. I told you I haven't been able to keep up with it for fear I could be traced through it. Last time I looked I was worth about . . . twenty-six."

"Twenty-six what? Twenty-six dollars? Twenty-six hundred? Twenty-six thousand?"

"Million."

When he didn't say anything she finally looked up at him. In the light cast by the lamp beside the back door she could see the stunned surprise on his face. "Why? How much are you worth?"

"A little more than that. But it never occurred to me..." He shook his head. "Do you mean to tell me that all the while you've worked odd jobs to support yourself and had to barter for places to stay, you could have been living in the lap of luxury?"

"We didn't barter for places to stay," she corrected peevishly. "I told you before that we performed a service as house sitters."

For a moment he just stared at her, as if seeing her for the first time. "You really are something special, do you know that?"

"Does that mean you're going to let me push you into the pool now?"

"Not a chance." He seemed to have recovered his wits. His grin was broad as he laced one arm across her shoulders and took her into the house. "The other reason I dunked you was that when I opened my shower curtain this morning and saw you sitting there looking like a drowned rat all I could think about was peeling off that robe and making love to you. This was just a way of reliving the moment."

"There had to have been an easier way" was the last thing she said as he pulled her into his bedroom, into his arms and found her mouth with his.

They made love quickly, urgently, a reaffirmation of each wanting the other in spite of all that had temporarily separated them. And when their reunion was sealed Patrick held Mitch in his arms, one leg thrown over hers protectively, as if he meant to impart to her that nothing like what she had been through would ever touch her again.

"I really am sorry about accusing you of using Hilly and my situation to your advantage," she said to him, her voice genuine and husky from passion. "I realized when I thought about it that that wasn't something you would do.''

"Apology accepted," he whispered into her hair. "And I wasn't actually doubting you when you popped in through the bathroom window this morning. I was just frustrated and madder than hell at you."

"I thought you couldn't think about anything but making love to me?" she teased him.

"That, too." He kissed the top of her head. "No more secrets?"

"I don't have any. How about you?"

"Maybe just one—I'm really impressed by you, Michelle Marie Cuddington. I knew you were a special lady but giving up all you did for Hilly, and going through what you have for the past few years for her sake leaves me speechless. I'd feel honored if you'd marry me, and lucky to have you on my side."

"Only on the condition that there are no more highhanded tactics like this morning's threat to do the article whether I cooperated or not."

"I was only trying to do what I thought was best for you."

"Even then."

"It's a deal. But I'm giving you fair warning that I think Hilly's son's false accusations and blackmail should be exposed. I'm going to put everything I have into convincing the two of you to let me launch *Probe* with that angle of the story."

"And if Hilly doesn't want you to?"

"I'll look under every rug that guy has until I find something else to expose him for. Everything that goes around comes around, you know, and if I can't get him for what he's done to you and Hilly I'll get him for something else."

"What if Hilly doesn't want you to do that, either?"

"I guess I'll pout."

"But will you print it?"

He seemed to think about that for a minute. "Maybe not as long as Hilly's around to see it. But I'm going to get him sooner or later."

"But you won't do it against Hilly's wishes now?"

"I thought you said you trust me?"

"I do, I do."

He chuckled. "Just the words I want to hear. So how about it? Marry me?"

"I think I can handle that."

He sighed contentedly. "It took a pretty bizarre path, but I believe this whole thing happened so we could find each other."

Mitch craned her head back to look up at him. "Now that's egotism. You think everything Hilly and I have been through was some design of fate to get me here to you?"

"Yep."

"Couldn't we just have met at a convention and still lived happily ever after?"

"Dues, Mitch, it was all paying dues. And now that they're paid we can go on forever."

It was the first time in a long, long while that Mitch actually believed she could have a forever. And a happy one at that. She breathed a full, deep, replete sigh. "I can handle that, too."

"And how about three kids and a draft horse of a dog with two stand-in grandparents living right next door?"

"Sounds perfect to me."

"Me, too," he whispered into her hair just before he tipped her chin and found her mouth with his once again.

\* \* \* \* \*

# Silhouette Special Edition

## COMING NEXT MONTH

**#601 LOVE FINDS YANCEY CORDELL—Curtiss Ann Matlock**
Yancey Cordell had every reason to be cynical about Annalise Pardee. Yet the fragile new ranch owner inspired a strange kind of loyalty... and evoked something suspiciously like love.

**#602 THE SPIRIT IS WILLING—Patricia Coughlin**
Thrust into an out-of-body experience, Jason Allaire landed the unlikely role of guardian angel to adorable oddball Maxi Love. But would earthy masculine urges topple his halo and destroy his second chance at love?

**#603 SHOWDOWN AT SIN CREEK—Jessica St. James**
LaRue Tate wasn't about to let the government commandeer her precious prairieland. But when ''government'' fleshed out as handsome, rakish J. B. Rafferty, she faced an unexpected showdown—with her own bridling passions!

**#604 GALAHAD'S BRIDE—Ada Steward**
Horseman Houston Carder had a heart the size of Texas, with more than enough room for sheltering delicate Laura Warner. But this particular damsel seemed to resist rescue, no matter how seductive the Sir Galahad!

**#605 GOLDEN ADVENTURE—Tracy Sinclair**
The thrill of being romanced by a mysterious expatriate made it worth missing her boat. Or so thought stranded traveler Alexis Lindley... until she discovered the dashing adventurer was a wanted man.

**#606 THE COURTSHIP OF CAROL SOMMARS—Debbie Macomber**
Cautious Carol Sommars successfully sidestepped amorous advances—until her teenage son rallied his best buddy, who rallied *his* sexy single dad, whose fancy footwork threatened to halt the single mom's retreat from romance....

## AVAILABLE THIS MONTH:

**#595 TEA AND DESTINY**
Sherryl Woods

**#596 DEAR DIARY**
Natalie Bishop

**#597 IT HAPPENED ONE NIGHT**
Marie Ferrarella

**#598 TREASURE DEEP**
Bevlyn Marshall

**#599 STRICTLY FOR HIRE**
Maggi Charles

**#600 SOMETHING SPECIAL**
Victoria Pade

# Indulge a Little
# Give a Lot

---

### A LITTLE SELF-INDULGENCE CAN DO
### A WORLD OF GOOD!

Last fall readers indulged themselves with fine romance and free gifts during the Harlequin®/Silhouette® "Indulge A Little—Give A Lot" promotion. For every specially marked book purchased, 5¢ was donated by Harlequin/Silhouette to Big Brothers/Big Sisters Programs and Services in the United States and Canada. We are pleased to announce that your participation in this unique promotion resulted in a total contribution of *$100,000.*

*

*Watch for details on Harlequin® and Silhouette®'s next exciting promotion in September.*

# A BIG SISTER
## can take her places

**She likes that. Her Mom does too.**

 **HARLEQUIN SUPPORTS BIG SISTERS**
For more information, contact your local Big Brothers/Big Sisters agency

## BIG BROTHERS/BIG SISTERS AND HARLEQUIN

Harlequin is proud to announce its official sponsorship of Big Brothers/Big Sisters of America. Look for this poster in your local Big Brothers/Big Sisters agency or call them to get one in your favorite bookstore. Love is all about sharing.

BB/BS 1A